AF481471

As authors, we write our woes, our hopes, and our dreams. At the end of the day, it is a select few who stand beside us as creatives. Those friends who set themselves apart in our lives and support us and our words, our creativity, and our passion. This one's for Catrina, best friend to one of our contributors who passed away just before the release of this collection.

May she forever rest in peace.

FOREWORD

Thank you for picking up Supernatural Drabbles of Dread! If you don't know what a drabble is, it is typically defined as a piece of flash fiction of no more than one-hundred words. Let me tell you, it is harder than it sounds!

In this collection, we have given our authors the task of writing supernatural horror that is no more than two-hundred and fifty words. These stories are bite-sized but pack quite a punch! These are **horror** stories so reader, beware.

So, buckle in and enjoy....

Supernatural Drabbles of Dread

(Book Three in the Drabbles of Dread Collection)

xx

Macabre Ladies

AWAKE BY MCKENZIE RICHARDSON

Another fire in California. A murder in the next town. Protests, babies born, an engagement. I scroll past it all, seeing then instantly forgetting.

The screen of my phone glows against the darkness of another sleepless night. *One more minute*, I think to myself as I turn on my side, phone extending over the edge.

Something grabs my wrist. Startled, the phone slips from my grip, the still-lit screen illuminating the clenched hand squeezing my skin. It's connected to a long, knobby arm protruding from under the bed.

"Get off your phone," a rasping voice says. "You're keeping me awake."

AMUSING BY DAVID SIMMS

"You're the muse?"

The buxom blonde slashed an arm that ended in a talon across Lauran's chest. Blood streaked across his desk, dotting his notebooks, laptop, and coffee mugs.

The muse grinned. "*Got your attention? Pain arouses the soul. Can't expect to yank the story from you without your synapses firing white-hot.*"

"But how?" The failed writer cried on the floor, balled tight, grasping himself.

"*There's no time,*" it replied. "*Do you want to be a writer or not?*" Silvery eyes flashed love and mischief.

Lauran nodded and pulled himself into his chair.

"The story. It's stuck. My friends," he said, heaving, "Their books seem to flow from their minds through their fingers. Deals. Movies." He turned to stare into its now kaleidoscopic eyes.

The muse grinned once more. "*Write.*"

When he hesitated, it struck again, and again. Lauran howled into the emptiness of his apartment.

The words began to flow, a rusted faucet that something cranked open. Visions whirled of the plot unfurling. The characters whispered in his ears. The muse morphed into various beings, people, sexes, yet always returning to the form which seduced him best.

For days, weeks, months, the muse poked, prodded, stabbed, and defiled him, tearing the story from him, churning it from mental feces into a literary jewel.

When she pressed submit on his laptop, the writer lay broken and scarred across the floor.

"*See ya soon,*" she smiled, closing the door behind her. "*There's another book inside.*"

He raised a shaking finger. "Call me."

TWO OUT OF THREE BY B. A. NIELSON

Death and Lucifer sat on a street bench in front of an apartment building.

Death had an appointment with a Jumper, her first for the day, while Lucifer was eager to settle a bet.

A scattering of birds caught their attention, and they both looked up in time to see a middle-aged man dressed in a suit, plummet to earth, landing bluntly on the sidewalk in front of them.

"See!" said Death, "I told you they don't all come apart on impact."

Well, I'll be damned, mused Lucifer.

But, he wasn't convinced.

"Best two out of three buys lunch..."

THE JOB FROM HELL BY LANCE DALE

Since the day I started making memories, I knew I wanted to be a demon. I just imagined myself surfing on a lake of fire, flexing my bulging red muscles, and striking fear in the hearts of every living thing. It was the ultimate level of respect.

In order to achieve this goal, I needed to live a life of sin. No problem. I went around being as mean as possible. I never put away my shopping carts. I pissed all over the seats of public restrooms. I never used my turn signal. I was proof you didn't need to kill anyone to be a dark stain on humanity. I spread misery wherever I went.

When the day finally came for me to meet my judgment, I was ecstatic. I took the elevator down and handed my resume to the demon at the gate.

"I'm ready for a job," I said.

He popped on a pair of spectacles and eyed it over. Then he looked up at me with a disapproving stare. My heart sank.

"You're not evil. You're just an asshole. I have the perfect job for a piece of shit like you." he said.

So, here I am in this fucking doll's body. That's right. I'm a possessed doll. No muscles. No fire surfing. It's the same shit every time. I'm given to a family. I move around a bit. Their kids act creepy. They get rid of me. The cycle repeats. This is the definition of hell.

A NEW HOME
BY RADAR
DEBOARD

Lethotop had been living in the space, the void between worlds for far too long. He had floated in the ever expanding emptiness and had grown desperate for a way out.

It took years of patience, but he finally found a way to slip free. His essence jumped through a crack in the barrier between worlds. Hurled from the void,

Lethotop found himself being dropped onto a hardwood floor, with a stationary object sitting mere inches from him.

With utter excitement, Lethotop reached his monstrously shaped hands up to feel the child, snug in their bed.

"I'm home," he whispered.

FROM LIGHT TO DARK BY GEMMA PAUL

She looks up at him, the beast she is about to become, the right-hand man of Hades himself, the lord of the underworld, and his foot soldier, Cerillius, the dark angel. One who was once like her, a beacon of light from the heavens who fell from grace with an almighty thump.

She looks up at him, with his tall stature, handsomely chiseled face, his black charred skin with that hypnotic orange glow beneath, his spiral horns that stretch up high, and his magnificent black wings that make him hauntingly beautiful. Her back burns as she looks at those wings, the pain of hers being ripped away flashing through her mind.

Angelica knows she shouldn't do it, knows she

shouldn't give in and become a force of darkness, another foot soldier for Hades, but she so yearns to have her wings back. Even if these ones would be black as hell rather than white like the heavens. If ripping the souls from the living is the price she has to pay to be able to fly again, then so be it.

She kneels before him, Hades, as he places his hand on her forehead. She screams in agony as he seers his brand into her skin, watching as her skin turns black, and her back tears itself open pushing out her new wings like a mother baring a child.

From light to dark, from heaven to hell, from white to black, as she becomes the new foot soldier of death.

LEARNING RUSSIAN BY B.F. VEGA

"No, *Bah-Bah* is a grandmother. *Baba* is a head-scarf."

The man, bound with a nice thick chain, looked at me in confusion. I could tell that his American ears couldn't hear the difference, though we had been working at it for over a day now.

"Okay, one more time. How do you say head-scarf?"

"I say it and you let me go right?" He whined

"I swear it on my grandmother." I smiled at him.

His eyes closed and I could see the sweat beading on his high brow.

"Bah-bah," he said.

"Damn. I'm sorry. Well, since you clearly want my grandmother..." I turned and called into the woods around the clearing, "Baba Yaga. I've brought a gift."

Tall bony legs separated from the ring of trees and my grandmother squatted down to see him better.

"He will make a good stew," she said as she sniffed him with her long pointy nose.

The man started screaming, causing my grandmother to laugh.

"You are the best of my grandchildren," Baba Yaga said and handed me the sacrificial blade.

The ornate Emerald dagger flashed in the moonlight. It was essential to kill him correctly so that his spirit could be bound to my grandmother and so that his blood was not wasted as it made the best sausage.

"Please, no!" He pleaded

"You signed up for ultimate immersion lessons. Time to become immersed." I answered sweetly, as I plunged the dagger into his heart.

NEVER GO BACK TO THE SCENE OF THE CRIME BY JOSHUA E. BORGMANN

I was bored, so I kept stalking Cassandra's Face-book account. It was still up after two years, and while the posts had mostly died away, there were still a few friends posting. Most of it was "Miss you" or "I love you" messages, but a couple of people posted about memories they made with her. It was pathetic how they kept trying to keep her alive, but I kept coming back to her page night after night.

I was drunk when I finally posted. Nine shots of Jim Beam cleared the way for me to post: "*So what's it like being dead?*" I probably passed out a few minutes later, and by the time I woke up, there were a string of replies telling me to "respect the dead." Her mother called me "a scumbag" and claimed that her daughter would still be here if it wasn't for me. I laughed a lot thinking about that.

Later, I got a Messenger notification claiming to be from Cassandra. Some loser playing a joke on me, but I opened it and read, "Thanks for asking, babe. If you're really curious, come to the place where you left me, and I'll show you."

When I went to the field where I'd shot her seventeen times, she was waiting there.

"Glad you came, babe," she whispered as she took my hand. "Let me show you how it feels."

Her spirit left me there just as dead, cold, and lonely as I'd left her.

THE RETURN BY MEERA DANDEKAR

I walked the empty road, darkness swimming around me. I knocked twice and she opened the door.

"I'm home."

Her pained expression made me feel guilty.

"I'm sorry. I won't be late next time." She looked tired, aged. She had grown silver strands around the crown of her head. I restrained from touching her wrinkle lines.

I was only gone for a few hours.

She did not smile. I felt her gaze on my back as I walked away to clean up.

At dinner, no one spoke.

"Mom?" She looked up, not touching her food. I

didn't say anything.

My bedroom was empty. I touched the hard-wood floors as I sat in the middle of the room.

"Mom, where is all my stuff?"

She leaned against the door frame. "We gave it away. Twenty years ago."

She walked closer and caressed my face. Her hand felt hot against my skin. "You haven't aged a bit since we last saw you."

THE RISING BY MIKE DEADY

She awoke at the bottom of the stairs.

She remembered the vampire entering her bedroom and draining her blood. The vampire had then thrown her down the stairs head-first to break her neck, in order to prevent her from arising. Somehow, he had failed, and her spine was intact.

She jumped up.

"My baby!"

She ran up the stairs and into the baby's room. He was lying in his crib unharmed, sleeping peacefully.

Overwhelmed with relief that the vampire had left without feeding on her baby too, she picked him up.

He was so small. And she was so thirsty.

THE DEVIL IN PRINT BY N.M. BROWN

Having been an avid purveyor of books since childhood, I jumped at the chance to open my own bookstore. It used to be the joy of my life, until the day I met... him

He never told me his name, only came in inquiring if we promoted local authors. The name used on the cover was a pseudonym and he asked for no money, only permission to display it on the shelves. There was a plainness about him, rendering him unremarkable in almost every way.

It was easy to tell by the cover that it was a horror novella. The silhouette of a woman's screaming face was illuminated by a demon of fire. It intrigued me instantly, and my eyes began devouring the pages. It contained everything I loved in a book, suspense, sinister mystery, and tragedy. It was told from a detective's point of view as he investigated a string of mysterious deaths by fire. The medical examiner ruled them all as medical impossibilities, citing spontaneous combustion as the cause of death.

The story stayed with me, especially since I woke up to the wail of fire sirens three weeks later. Fourteen men, women and children burned to death in their beds on the same exact night with no signs of foul play or explanation.

The reason I'm writing this is because all those weeks ago, the man said something to me on his way out. He said, "Let me know if you like it. I've written dozens more."

SPIRITED AWAY
BY JOHN CADY

A group of us stood there, waiting to cross. The only one not standing was the homeless man, sitting there, possibly asleep. I couldn't tell. His head was down.

The little girl standing beside me seemed just as out of place. That is to say, she didn't look as though she belonged to anyone there. Her red balloon sort of stuck out as well. Perhaps I just wasn't accustomed to seeing children clutching balloons anymore. It always seemed like a thing of the past.

Within seconds, her balloon had taken on the image of a skull. Before I could make any sense of this transformation, she released it and it ascended wobbly into the sky, turning this way and that as a balloon might. It was then that the homeless man slumped over, and the crosswalk was ours.

RUNNING BY KIM PLASKET

Footsteps in the dark. When you turn on the light, there is nobody there. It's as if what is in the dark vanishes in the light unless it is invisible like most undead creatures are. Familiar places become scary when the darkness arrives. You sense there is someone, or something, there, but your senses seem to fail you.

You wait for the crack of the gun or the sting when the blade rips into your skin. There is nothing other than a small chill that travels up your spine. You shake off the feeling as your imagination.

A bony hand grabs you by the shoulder and spins you around. The smell of death and decay greets you like an old friend. You can finally see what had been stalking you and you immediately wish you could go back to unseeing.

Flesh falls from the bone. Tattered remains of clothing hanging onto the bones after decay. Maggots squirm where the eyes once were, skeletal hands grip you tight and it pulls you closer.

"Come home, my love," as you tumble into the grave you had been running from.

BETTER THAN CURSES BY JOSH DARLING

Both women peered out from behind the curtains at the teenaged boy in the front yard holding a 1-gallon red plastic gasoline can.

"Catherine," he shouted.

"Catherine," her mother said, "I thought I told you to curse that little shit incel before we moved five hundred miles away from him."

"I did something better, I put a love spell on him."

"I don't understand, you wanted him to lust after you?"

"No, I wanted him to know the pain of yearning, buy me a bunch of stuff, and then do something like this."

"Like what?"

Catherine opened the window, "Prove your love to me, show me how much you're willing to sacrifice."

He raised the can above his head. When nothing came out, he lowered it, unscrewed the cap, then began dowsing himself.

"My life for you."

"This way I'm not putting any negative energy out into the world."

"Wow, Catherine, I don't know if this is a total abuse of magic or genius."

"I'm going with genius, I am your daughter."

He pulled a cheap gas station lighter from his pants pocket.

"When you light yourself on fire, run into my neighbor's yard."

Mother's brow lowered, "*Catherine Janet Montgomery.*"

"You said they let their dog poop in our yard all the time."

With a flash, they felt the heat of ignition.

RENOVATIONS: PART ONE BY GARY MCDONOUGH

It was after three hard months of renovations before Reece unearthed the skull in a wall cavity in his 12th-century medieval manor house. While removing an internal wall to create more living space on the first floor, he made the gruesome discovery and called the police. Forensics respectfully removed the skull after a police investigation, although the body was never located.

A little over a week passed before Detective Crawley returned to Morley's Hall carrying a cardboard box under his arm.

"May I come in, Mr. Cottam? I have a serious

matter to discuss." The detective had worry etched across his face.

Reece made tea and invited Detective Crawley to take a seat at the kitchen table. Pushing a pile of papers to one side, he placed the box in the center of the table and took a seat.

"What I'm about to share with you may give you grounds to think I have lost my mind," stated the Detective. "Since removing the head from your abode it hasn't stopped screaming."

Reece wanted to laugh, there were so many things wrong with that sentence. It couldn't possibly be true; a lack of lips, lungs, and vocal cords, not to mention a body and being dead made this scientifically impossible. He must be joking. Yet Detective Crawley's grave expression never waned.

MYTH BY DOUG HAWLEY

A bunch of them broke into my home shouting gibberish while I was sleeping.

In the dark, there was no way to get a good look at them, but they were some kind of aliens or monsters. I tried to get them to leave, but they pointed odd-looking weapons at me. They gave me no choice but to fire my body lasers at them.

When I shined a light on their bodies, I discovered they had some sort of fur at the top, were covered with artificial skin, and had only four appendages.

Until now, I thought humans were a myth about savage creatures told by elders to scare us when we were young, but the bodies were exactly as they described. This is the scientific discovery of our age. Too bad that I couldn't get any live ones to examine.

ONE OF US BY SERENA JAYNE

The metallic tang of the blood Clive had forced Nina to drink filled her sinuses. Her body practically hummed as the virus murdered her cells before infusing them with unholy life.

She found both their bodies in the kitchen, side by side on the orange linoleum. Clive's skin bore the same mottled purple blotches as the vampire she'd injected to test the poison. A knife handle protruded from Liam's chest, and blood stained his shirt.

She kicked the vampire aside and started chest compressions on her lover. Liam's lips were stiff, but she managed to pry them open to force air into his unresponsive lungs.

The words rigor and mortis came to mind, but she refused to acknowledge their meaning. Her world narrowed to Liam's citrus scent, the chill of his waxen skin, his lack of vital signs.

A hand closed around her ankle.

She grabbed the closest weapon.

With a sickening slurp, the blade came free of Liam's skin. She stabbed at the master vampire and stuck her last syringe of the drug into the fiend's flesh for good measure.

There was only one way out of her hell hole.

Holding Liam's hand, she shuffled into the sliver of tile illuminated by sunlight.

When her skin started to sizzle, she yanked her hand away. The blood on her lips was ambrosia. She swore she wouldn't become like Clive and his murderous minions. But as she waited for day to turn to night, her relentless thirst told her otherwise.

IN A SITUATION WITHOUT AN EXIT BY CHRISTOPHER T. DABROWSKI

Trapped in something soft, warm, he felt he had to free himself. Especially since he was already very hungry. He did not know how long he was herE but judging by the increasing drooling, for a long time. He started struggling. His body was covered in mucus as if the prison was a living thing, warm and enveloping.

He's getting out of here!

From words to deeds. He bit through soft walls.

He finally saw the bright light.

He bit more holes and heard screams. He saw a strange box. In it, his brother was getting closer to the woman's face....

COFFIN MATES
BY TERRY MILLER

I had a dream that I walked amongst the dead. I awoke, my body shivering as if I brought the cold out with me. My limbs were stiff and the room was dark and damp. Attempting to move, I banged both my elbows; the sudden, numbing pain being anything but humorous.

Panicking, I found myself surrounded on every side, and the air I frantically breathed grew thin. Fingers clawed at my shirt, ripping it bottom to top. My stomach soured as rank breath exhaled onto my face. Something had followed me back, its frigid, bony fingers slipping under my skin.

ASYLUM BY NERISHA KEMRAJ

Hannah shut her eyes, avoiding the dark corner where the croaking stemmed from.

"You're not real. You're not real. They said you're not real." She rocked back and forth on the bed.

Reopening her eyes, she saw the demon standing before her; eyes glowing with rage.

She screamed as he grabbed her throat, flinging her across the room.

Grabbing her again, he smashed her head against the door, repeatedly, bloodying the tiny glass window.

He only let go when the nurses entered.

"How did she free herself? Restrain her! A third

suicide attempt in three days!"

Hannah succumbed to sedation.

THE BUBAK BY GEMMA PAUL

"I know what I heard," she says as she fights her way through the field of corn that stands a good arm's length above their heads reaching up into the night sky.

"I just asked why a baby would be all the way out here?" he replies as he follows after her trying to prevent being smacked in the face by the corn she brushes aside.

The cry of a baby rings out once more, Jane and Duncan both stopping in their tracks.

"Ok, I heard it that time," Duncan says as Jane starts running through the field towards the crying child. She keeps going, fighting the corn as the baby's cries get louder. Coming to an abrupt stop she finds herself in a small opening looking up at a withered scarecrow perched atop a stake in the ground.

The baby cries again as Duncan practically crashes into her back.

"Where is it?" he asks looking around as the sound suddenly stops.

"I don't know, it should be here," she says unable to tear her eyes away from the figure made of straw with a black cloak flapping in the breeze and a felt blue hat perched upon its head. The figure that lifts itself up off its stake, picks up a scythe from the ground and slices her in two.

Duncan screams and runs, leaving Jane's right side of her body flopping to the ground in a bloody heap, her left following seconds later.

KARMA BY MARIE STERLING

All she can do is watch. Watch as the guests offer their hugs and condolences to him, the grieving husband. Watch as their children gather around their father in this time of shared sorrow. Watch as the man she vowed to love and honor until death do them part brings his business partner around to meet their son and daughter.

She can still feel his hands on her shoulders, holding her down beneath the water of her bubble bath. Feel her lungs struggle for air, chest burning. Then nothing. Nothing until this new existence of watching her family's life from the outside. Her daughter's first boyfriend. Her son's first car, bought with part of the insurance payout from her death. The shiny new wedding bands on the fingers of her husband and his business partner, now wife.

Watch and wait is all she does, until one day she sees the new wife slip a special ingredient into the man's nightly bourbon. Sees him smile and take a sip and begin choking. Sees the woman smile back and do nothing as the man gasps out his last and slumps back in his chair. Then the new wife turns and looks at the corner where the previous wife stands, silent and invisible. She is still smiling.

"You're welcome."

IMPRINTED BY N.M. BROWN

One of the hardest things I've ever had to do as a mother and human being was explain to my eight-year-old son Cody that he'd never see his sister Jade again.

Tensions were high from being cooped in the house. She and Cody had been bickering all day. My husband took her out for ice cream to separate them for a bit and cheer her up. We lost her at only four years old in a horrific car accident that took place on the way home.

Her brother was inconsolable for months. I think in a way, he heartbreakingly blamed himself. He said wished he hadn't been nasty to her that day and asked me if I thought she knew that he was sorry. It was no surprise when he started acting out and things began…changing.

I'd find him in Jade's room in the middle of the

night. He'd be fast asleep in her bed, clutching her favorite stuffed animals. My husband worried when he tried wearing the clothes she had that were too big for her and started sitting down to pee. I wasn't too worried; grief comes in many forms especially in the minds of small children.

Cody ritualized watching her favorite shows and his speech patterns regressed. I began to worry when he would reference Jade's memories that he had no knowledge of.

My fears were confirmed one morning when he spoke in her voice, "The transfer's all done, Mommy."

WITHIN THESE WALLS BY NERISHA KEMRAJ

They've since moved me from Solitary. Things have been quiet for a while.

Nobody believes that he came back for me. And he'll never stop until he takes me. They still think it was an attempted suicide.

"Maybe they're right, and I'm losing my mind," I say to Jenny who occupies the room adjacent to mine.

"Well, you're locked up in this nuthouse, aren't you?!" She laughs.

And then I hear him. The demon's sinister laugh creeps in from within the white walls.

"Nurse! He's back! He's here, again! Help me!" I scream as I back away from him.

"No, Hannah. You aren't losing your mind. I am here. I've always been here." His fiery eyes burn into me as he suspends me in mid-air, twirling the bedsheet around my neck. "Time to have a little fun, hey."

My eyes are ready to burst out of my head and I feel the pressure rising on my face as the sheet winds tighter.

"Just kill me, already!" I manage, as he toys with me.

"But, darling, you know you can't have the easy way out!" He smiles as his claws slice thin slivers across my arms, relishing the joy at the sight of my blood. *I will not scream.*

I fall, as Jenny's cries for help, grow fainter.

THE THRILL OF BATTLE BY SCOTT MCGREGOR

In the depths of night, two knights clashed in the wasteland of Kalifa, swords singing the rhythm of battle. Beaten and bruised, Teriff studied Lucio's every move, not a scratch on his armour.

"You can't defeat me, Teriff," Lucio mocked.

Teriff smiled, chanting the passage necessary for his trump card.

"Grilz py wa Sul calio aly!"

Then, Terrif grew thrice his size. Black wings burst through his armour, and his skin turned the colour of red wine. His eyes shifted to the glow of greenish-yellow, and his razor-sharp fangs emerged, lips bloody. He dropped his sword, no longer needing a blade to win the duel. Soon enough, this encounter would no longer be a duel at all, but a slaughter.

When Teriff saw the dread painted on his opponent's face, his hunger stirred.

This is what enraged him.

This is what empowered him.

The thrill of battle, and the flesh he'd feast upon after.

WITCHCRAFT FOR DUMMIES BY WONDRA VANIAN

"Um… excuse me?"

The Priestess stopped mid-invocation. She threw back her black hood with an angry flick of the wrist not holding a dagger.

"Fool!" she snapped. "Do you have any idea how dangerous it is to interrupt a sacrifice?"

The man tied to the alter cleared his throat. "Well…" he admitted, "No. I mean, this is my first."

A white-robed initiate stepped forward. "*Witchcraft for Dummies* says it's customary to gag the sacrifice," he offered without being asked.

Another figure threw back her purple hood. "This is why nepotism has no place in a coven," she complained loudly. "Just because your grandmother is High Priestess..." Scowling, she rounded on the initiate.

"Alright," the Priestess snapped. "Everyone just calm down..."

She leaned over the bound man. "You, what did you want to say?"

"Oh. Only that my hand is free..."

In a flash of movement, the sacrifice grabbed the black-handled knife from the Priestess's hand and buried it deep in her throat. With a gurgle, she fell back, dead.

The others stared in mute shock as the sacrifice used the bloody knife to cut through the remaining ropes. He slid off the marble altar, bent to tug the black robe free from the Priestess's corpse, shook it out, and shrugged it on.

"Right," he said, taking her place, "we'll need a new sacrifice."

All eyes turned to the initiate.

The other purple-robed woman lifted the hood back over her head.

"Don't forget to gag him," she said with a grin.

CAN I KEEP THE DOG BY JOSHUA E. BORGMANN

The dog has been acting weird. It won't stop looking at me. I feed it constantly, but it just looks at the bowl for a few seconds before turning its gaze back on me. I tried replacing the kibble with fresh steak, fucking top sirloin, but the damn dog wouldn't eat. It started growling at me like I was a complete stranger. It'd never done that before.

It's been hard to adapt to my new state, but the change is just too much for the dog to handle. It keeps licking my dead body while I'm standing right beside it.

SPIRITS BY M ENNENBACH

"It says Milton Fucking Bradley on the box." Cassie shook the empty box.

"Who cares?" Eleanor said, shrugging.

"Are we really doing this?" Ruthanne looked none too pleased by any of the shenanigans.

Eleanor got up and flipped the light switch and the room dimmed to the flickering candles burning on the tables. "Yes."

Cassie lit a joint off of the nearest candle and took a long drag while managing also roll her eyes in a near-epic fashion. She passed it to Ruthanne who took a hit while staring anxiously at the board. Eleanor gleefully set the planchette down and took the joint with a grin.

"Everyone gently set your fingers on the planchette, I'll ask the questions," Cassie announced. Eleanor let out a healthy cloud of smoke and nodded.

"This is stupid," Ruthanne declared, unconvin-cingly.

"Yo, spirit bitches! Anyone there?" Cassie asked. Nothing. "Don't be scared, we are good witches."

The planchette slid to No.

"You do that?" Ruthanne asked.

Each of them went a shade paler.

"Are you ghosts?"

No.

Ruthanne gulped hard. "Demons?"

No.

"What are you?" Eleanor asked.

A-L-I-V-E

"The fuck? We know we are alive, idiot. What are you?" Cassie asked.

K-I-D-S

"Smartass. Fine kids, what year is it?" Cassie spat.

2-0-2-0

"Ha! It's 1985, dumbass!" Eleanor yelled.

A-U-N-T-C-A-S-S-I-E-?

Cassie squeaked, "What the fuck?"

T-H-E-K-I-L-L-E-R-C-A-M-E-B-A-C-K-W-E-H-A-D-F-O-U-N-D-Y-O-U-R-O-L-D-O-U-I-

Ruthanne pulled her hands away. "No! This is insane! What killer came back?"

That was when they heard the front door click shut and the sound of shoes slowly climbing the staircase.

THE LONG WALK BY MIRIAM H. HARRISON

Her shoes walked about at night. She could hear them pace through the house all night, yet by morning they always returned to their place by the door, waiting for her.

One morning she came down to find the shoes dirty. More than dirty—ruined. The once-white sneakers were caked with mud, scratched as if from underbrush. She went through the house and found the back door standing open.

That night, she brought the shoes to her bedroom and set them down beside her bed. Closing the bedroom door, she settled into bed.

It wasn't long before her shoes began to shuffle

about, then pace the room. She rose and opened the door. The shoes hurried out; she followed close behind. Down the hall, the stairs, to the front door. The shoes shuffled about eagerly as she turned the latch, opened the door. They hurried out, but she hesitated at the threshold, her feet bare.

The shoes returned, organized themselves at her feet, waited. She slipped her feet inside. Before she could close the door behind her, the shoes had already carried her into the night.

The door stood open through the night, the morning, into the afternoon. It was only then that a neighbor came by. He poked his head inside, concerned. He pulled his head back, frightened.

There, by the door, were her shoes. They were ragged from their long walk. Torn, scratched by stones and underbrush, they sat there. Stained through and through with blood, they waited.

OLD MOTHER CRITCHLEY'S PLACE BY RAINIE ZENITH

Old Mother Critchley's place had stood empty as long as I could remember. She died before I was born, but my parents had told me stories about the strange old woman who dressed in black and never left the house. She had an extensive herb garden, and rumor had it she was a witch.

Being a reclusive green thumb sounded more like typical old woman behavior to me, but who am I to say? I never knew her.

Jed and I were out trick or treating last Halloween when we knocked at Old Mother Critchley's house as a joke. We had to beat our way through the long-neglected garden to reach the dilapidated cobweb-swathed cottage.

Imagine our surprise when a young lady in black answered the door.

"Trick or treat!" Jed and I chorused.

She silently handed us two sour candies each.

I'm not a fan of the sour ones, so I gave mine to Jed, who of course gobbled them down straight away.

Half a minute later, his eyes rolled back and he collapsed in the road. Unable to rouse him, I called an ambulance.

Half an hour later, the paramedics pronounced him dead. Blood tests revealed he had been poisoned but was unable to identify by what kind of substance. I mentioned the sour candies and took them to Old Mother Critchley's place, but the house appeared entirely uninhabited.

THE TOY CHEST BY STEPHEN JOHNSON

John walked around the wooden chest admiring the antique quality. His daughter, Sally, gasped also admiring the aged chest.

"Daddy, this would be great for all my toys, don't you think? John laughed at his wife, Beth, and gave her a smile as he reached for his wallet.

After setting up Sally's toy chest, the family sat down to dinner. Sally excitedly devoured her food anxious to see how many toys could fit in the new chest. She ran upstairs and immediately opened the chest to examine it. Staring into the bottom of the chest she noticed a red-carpeted stairwell leading down into darkness. A raspy voice called up to her, "Come join us, there is so much to play with." Sally giggled and dashed down the stairwell.

Later that evening, John stopped in Sally's room and noticed the open chest but did not see Sally. He walked to the chest and panicked as he saw the stairwell. He heard his daughter cry out, "Daddy, come play with us." John rushed down the chest stairwell and it closed behind him.

A few hours later, Beth walked into her bedroom and noticed John was not there. She walked into Sally's room witnessing her daughter standing motionless in front of the chest staring down at a crude demonic carving and the walls covered in ancient symbols. Sally looked up with a sinister grin as the chest opened up, "Come play Mommy, Daddy has been waiting for you."

THE VEIL
BY WENDY
CHEAIRS

The clock ticked closer to the wolf hour. Ignored for the famous midnight as a "magical" hour, those in the know could use the correct magic time without bystanders. Another tick dropped, slowed with the magic swelling the circle within. The music from beyond the veil, the group had contacted beyond the veil. The chosen witch entered the ring to offer herself to finish the spell to cut the final space between here and there. She touched the waving space between the realms.

The bloody knife lifted, she could hear her coven, singing songs of their ancestors. She plunged the dagger deep into space. She twisted with her power, given to her by the ancients beyond what any human could muster just for this night to tear the veil asunder.

The ripping tore through the forest. It echoed throughout the world. The bloody shriek rolled through the world; nightmares followed.

It called; it awoke the ancient followers. They turned their attention to the waking maw from the void. The tentacles spilled from the void, the world between worlds. One grabbed the witch, pulling her into space, the opening to eat like the rest of the coven screamed.

Not knowing what they had done, what they had unleashed onto the world. This is not what they thought they had called. This was else, beyond the planets.

The void was here, and they could not stop it. They scattered, attempting to outrun the tendrils of the ancient forgotten gods they had awoken.

RENOVATIONS: PART 2 (THE SCREAMING SKULL) – BY GARY MCDONOUGH

Detective Crawley slowly removed the skull from the box in which it had been housed and placed it carefully on the table. He took a sip from his tea and placed his finger on top of the yellowing dome.

"This is the first time this thing has been quiet since we moved it away from here, screaming incessantly. Nighttime became intolerable; we had to alter shift patterns as officers refused to be in the building for sustained periods of time."

He spun it around and gazed into the empty eyes that stared back at him. Wanting it to tell him its story.

"And now looking like an insane arsehole, I'm carrying a skull around in a box. We consulted numerous specialists, priests, and such. They all suggested the same course of action, returning it here to its resting place till we learn more about it. Now, it's finally quiet, I'll take my leave, gain a peaceful night's sleep, and return when we know more!"

The detective rose wearily from his chair, drained his mug of tea, and let himself out via the side-door in the kitchen leaving an open-mouthed Reece alone with his new house guest.

A horrific cacophony woke Reece in the middle of the night, reverberating around the house were a multitude of screams; in his room, down-stairs, in the loft. Instantly, he knew where it emanated from. Bolting from his bed, bounding down to the kitchen he found the skull sitting where he left it.

HAMMERED BY GABRIELLA BALCOM

Glenn swung his hammer at the nail, missed and aimed a second time, but still didn't hit his target. He swayed on his feet, a deep belch escaping his mouth, and glared at the tool in his hand.

"Worthless piece of trash," he muttered. He threw it as hard as he could, sneering when it slammed into the kitchen floor, the wooden handle cracking.

After stumbling over to give it a contemptuous kick, he headed for the refrigerator, taking out a cold beer. It was one in a long line since he'd been drinking all day.

The tool rose, hovered in the air briefly, then slowly floated in Glenn's direction.

"What the…" He gasped but blanched as it

picked up speed, zooming toward him.

The hammer struck him and he yelled, "*Ow!*"

It began hitting him again and again, and he tried to evade it, but couldn't.

Within moments, Glenn lay motionless on the floor, his head a crushed, bloody mess.

HATCHED BY MIRIAM H. HARRISON

That night he hatched from her dreams—dripping, dribbling onto her pillow, her bed, her floor. He pooled there among dropped toys and forgotten socks, gathering himself to himself until at last he could squirm, slide into the deeper dark beneath her bed.

Above, she tossed, turned, scattering dark dreams into the air around her. Below, he breathed them in. He wrapped the dust bunnies and wayward socks close about him—gathering, gathering, until his cocoon was complete. There he would wait, drawing strength from her dark dreams. For now, they fed his hunger, but soon he would emerge—hungry for things darker still.

TEAR AT THE END OF THE WORLD BY DAVID SIMMS

Tina's grandmother always told her that she could see what others couldn't, what they refused to see.

Last Tuesday morning, after running away from the mean kids in her class, she sat on the curb in front of her little house and cried. Her mother and father remained inside, pretending not to hear anything.

That's when she noticed it. A small tear. At first, she thought it to be a scrap of paper caught in the wind or a dark feather stuck in the street. Yet when she rose and walked over to it, she realized what adults could never realize. A rip in the sky, or the curtain of her world, flapped like a hole in the seat of reality's pants.

She knelt on a skinned knee and peered inside. Her left eye turned gray immediately and she whistled, "that's not good." She pressed down the flapping piece of sky to halt what existed behind it from sneaking out.

For the next few nights, Tina dreamt of what lie beyond that tear. She woke up each day and smiled before pulling hold of the edge and ripping it a bit more, listening to them howl and skitter beyond.

On a Friday after a particularly bad day when she disliked everyone, she packed her lunchbox, walked to the tear, lifted it, and crawled inside to join the dark forces within.

Tina knew she would return soon to visit those who made her cry.

She'd bring her new friends to help.

ENSNARED BY NATASHA SINCLAIR

Emerging from the thicket, the mysterious stallion piqued the young stranger's curiosity as she dismounted from the tree-swing. Exuding a majestic, regal air, he bowed his great grey speckled muzzle and invited her to mount.

Running delicate fingers, dreamily, through the animal's dense mane, he trotted, gait quickening to a gallop —he had somewhere to be. Frankie's fingers became tangled in the hair, wrapping itself up her forearms in a furious whip, binding the child to his muscular body. A scream was stifled from the girl's lips as her body was sharply yanked forth, and her face pressed tight against his strapping neck.

The stallion grew large, his back widening between her legs. He grew in height, so the ground was now frightfully far from her small feet. His pace continued to quicken, branches whipped at her legs as the stallion holding her in bondage tore through the trees, towards the glass-still Loch.

The Kelpie broke the water with ease; the once perfectly serene Loch rippled, the wild landscape seemed to move with it, morphing into nightmare-like chaos. The girl's body trembled with an unbearable cold rising from her toes.

Ensnared by the water horse, she knew her fate, as his solid form grew monstrous, taking on the near-transparent, reflective surface of the water. His great neck elongated and his muzzle turned towards her, fire roared through his eyes, and he plunged, with the child, into the consuming depths. Free enough to finally scream, the water poured mercilessly down her throat.

ONE HIT WONDERBY SERENA JAYNE

Sebastian rubbed the shiny lamp.

Genie appeared. "Last wish."

"Immortality," Sebastian said. "'Sunshine Serenade' went platinum in '65, but the dawn of disco doomed my song to obscurity. Success doesn't last forever, but I can."

"Granted." Genie dissipated into a blue mist.

Sebastian's mouth ached. "How very underwhelming." Newly pointed teeth sliced his tongue.

His late-night snack of garlic-heavy pasta burned his belly. He craved blood.

The sunrise lit up his panoramic million-dollar view. On cue, 'Sunshine Serenade' played in surround sound.

He yelped, skin smoking. Darted away from the sunlight.

Lack of specificity would be the death of him.

RETURNING THE FAVOR BY SOPHIE WAGNER

"Why are you doing this!" He screamed as I sprinkled maggots into the casket I had put him in.

"Who are you!"

Briefly, I wondered how he did not remember me. Was I not the first person he had done this to?

"Do you know what it is like to be buried under the earth, slowly digested by the bugs you once squashed?" I whispered, "You stabbed me, you buried me. And when you buried me, you buried me alive. I'm just… returning the favor."

"Carmen? Aren't you dead?" He stuttered.

"Oh, yes. And soon, you will be too."

"Goodbye."

BROKEN BY B. A. NIELSON

Razor-sharp claws dug into his shoulders, bits of blood and flesh dripping from its open jaw. He shut his eyes waiting for it to tear him apart.

A gunshot rang through the room and the creatures' weight shifted from on-top of him.

Opening his eyes, above him stood his wife, a sawed-off shotgun in her hands.

She turned the gun around, revealing its broken handle as the creature lunged at her. It screamed when she drove the handle into its chest, bursting it into ash.

She turned to her husband, "Fuck, I hate vampires," was all she said.

MOLLY MALONE BY M. BETTERELLI

It was a foggy evening filled with moisture ladened sea sprays on the shores of Dublin. Molly walked through the streets yelling, "Mussels and cockles alive, alive, oh!"

The wheelbarrow filled with an array of mollusks was pushed through the muddy walkways, powered by its owner. Molly was as fair a fishmonger's daughter as she could've been. The whole town adored her. The normal call out of "Mussels and cockles alive, alive, oh!" usually brought out anyone who cared to buy the fresh catch of the day.

Tristan, a young man of eighteen, would visit Molly every day in hopes to brew up the courage of courting her. This went on for several months.

He never told his parents of his love for the woman, only because he didn't know if she'd except. He ran out into the evening to meet her as he always had, and promptly found her pushing her wheelbarrow.

"Ah, dare yer are. Oi' av somethin' oi want ter ask yer. Oi wud loike ter court yer, wud yer except?"

Molly nodded with a smile. Tristan blissfully planted a kiss upon her cheek and ran off to tell his parents.

Arriving at the house he stormed in spinning around smitten by love.

"Why ye so 'appy?" His mother asked.

"Oi asked Molly if oi cud court 'er, an' she said aye!" Tristan told his mother gleefully.

"Ah son, oi don't nu 'ow ter tell yer dis, but Molly doid av de fever, jist last noight."

THE GREATEST EXPLORER BY GEMMA PAUL

For years she has been searching, been following the path that will lead her to her destiny. She wanted to be the first, to have her name down in history books alongside Marco Polo and Christopher Columbus, as one of the greatest explorers of all time. Faith Griffin, the woman who found the pot of gold at the end of the rainbow.

As she kneels on the ground, gripping her wrist tightly trying to stem the flow of blood that spurts viciously out of the space her hand once occupied, she realizes there is a reason why no one has found it.

The creature before her giggles one of the most terrifying sounds she has ever heard. It's razor-sharp teeth dripping with her blood as it spits out her chewed fingers to land at her knees. She looks up at it once more, face wet with tears.

"Why?" she asks.

"No one steals from a Leprechaun," it says with a cackle as it lunges forward, teeth piercing her face as her screams echo off the hidden valley found at the end of the rainbow.

KNOCK ON WOOD BY MARY RAJOTTE

The otherworld seeps like mist through the thinning veil.

Match strikes offer hope with light and heat. Symbols scrawled in sand promise protection. Talismans burn with potential energy to ward off unlucky consequence.

The forest lingers in silhouette, coaxing me with whispered intent. My footfalls are subdued in grass thick and lush with dew as I approach the thicket. With my palm pressed to the oak, I listen.

Crickets fall silent. The wind dies away. And as the spirits approach, I rap my knuckles against the hardwood. Once. Twice. A third time for luck.

From deep within, something knocks back.

ALPHA BY MIRIAM H. HARRISON

Running through the moonlit forest, she could hear them howl. The sounds rang out in the cold, seeming to echo from tree to tree. She couldn't tell which direction they were coming from, but she knew that they were close.

Her lungs burned inside her, the cold air cutting icy pains with each breath. The snow beneath her hid roots and branches and other grabbing things that pulled at her boots. She was slowing.

They were not.

The howls sounded again. The first of them was clearer, closer. *The alpha*, she thought, her dread growing. The howl was near, so near, when it suddenly cut short in a series of yelps.

Then she heard it. A new sound rose above the desperate cries of the wolf. It was a deep sound, reverberating through the air, the trees, the very bones of her body.

She had feared the wolves, but now she was shaken more deeply by a terror she had never known. A fear that had no name. A fear that rose up on dark wings from the trees behind her, still all too hungry.

PARALYSED BY FEAR BY MARINA SCHNIERER

Draping slowly over my eyes like a warm blanket, my eyelids succumb to intense fatigue. I sink deeply into the mattress beneath me, its softness caressing me like a gentle, attentive lover. Residual tension dissipates as my mind and body drifts away to that comforting realm of sleep.

Buzzing fills my ears and vibrates in my head like thousands of angry bees. My eyes open; any attempt to move an impossible task. Am I dreaming?

Vile odors surround me, a gag-inducing mixture of festering, rotting meat, putrid fish, and toe fungus.

I desperately want to flee this motel room, but can't.

An enormous weight bears down on my chest, my lungs struggle for air. A hag-like creature floats above me, grinning, jagged teeth exposed, its fetid breath wafting directly into my nostrils. Bile reaches my throat and burns like acid.

I want to be sick, but can't.

I pray for this nightmare to end, if that's indeed what it is, but I'm not convinced, this feels too real.

As the weight on my chest becomes unbearable, and I feel my life slipping away, a gentle knocking on the door soon turns violent.

As the door creaks open, another figure comes into view. The unbearable weight on my chest lifts and the hag disappears. Finally able to sit up, I see my boss's face in the doorway.

Relief washes over me as she steps inside, but as the door slams closed, the vile odors return; my boss grinning, jagged teeth exposed.

TOP BUNK BY DAVID O. HUGHES

Toby stared up at the underside of the mattress, his nightlight illuminating it. The top bunk was only ever used for sleepovers.

"Have you been scratching yourself in your sleep again, son?" his dad asked.

"No. The burned boy did it. He lives in my bed."

Dad laughed at his childishness.

The springs above creaked.

Toby clutched his teddy bear and closed his eyes.

"Toby..." the scratchy voice called.

"No!" He looked, seeing the upside-down, chargrilled face of the boy above, his charcoaled hand reaching, his gnarled fingers searching.

"I'll take your soul to be a little boy again, Toby..."

VISITATION BY CHISTO HEALY

Cameron knew that someone was in the house with him. He awoke to the sound of glass shattering and things crashing to the floor on the first floor. He knew it wasn't a burglary. This was the third time it had happened.

Each time, he found no one; just his broken things, the front door open.

Cameron thought maybe it was a ghost, his late wife Brenda, but he couldn't figure why she would be so angry, destructive.

He made his way down the stairs to find the windows broken outward and the door splintered and taken off the hinges. As he stood before it, the room filled with blinding white light. He shielded his eyes against it, squinting through it as a silhouette appeared where his door had once been, the light bending around it. A thin arm reached through the light, long fingers grasping his arm.

Then it was over.

The figure was gone.

The light was gone.

Cameron was alone again in the destruction of his house, the house that hadn't felt like home since Brenda had left him. Now he had been visited and they left him too. Weeping, he stumbled past the wrecked door into the dark of the night, where he fell to his knees in the grass. Staring up at the stars, he cried, "Take me with you! Please! Come back! Take me with you!"

Silence answered him, but he knew they would come again.

BURIED GHOSTS BY JODIE FRANCIS

I believe there is nothing better than the sound of children's laughter. A tinkly, musical sound -it really does fill me with such joy! I could identify my child out of a line-up if I were blindfolded and told to simply listen to their laughter. Then I would scoop up my little angel and we would be together forever and ever!

It was difficult enough hiding him from his dad, I mean it's not like he bothered with Max before the divorce. I think he's just doing it to spite me. Shared custody, for goodness sake! Well, not much longer and I'll have my little Maxie all to myself. Trust Kane to try and pull the mental health card at the courts, didn't work now, did it? I'll show him.

More musical laughter from the garden. I smile to myself, as I went to spy on my little Maxie. You can imagine my surprise when I saw him playing with his little sister, though. Both of them skipping and running about the garden. How odd. I truly thought I had buried her deep enough this time. Never mind, we will all be together soon enough.

MALLARD LAKE BY B.F. VEGA

I should just move here, I think as I leave the SF State campus heading up Sunset toward the bridge. I try and hurry to get out of San Francisco before night falls. Usually, I take 19th and deal with traffic. Tonight, I have left too late. There is an accident blocking 19th.

It's stupid. The ghost stories are all associated with Stow Lake, not Mallard Lake. But it's Mallard that freaks me out. I tell myself that the misty shapes I always see are just fog forming over the cold water. I tell myself that my car drifting a little too close to the edge is just a misalignment. I tell myself that I should be more afraid of the treacherous and haunted waters of the Golden Gate. I tell myself a lot of things.

The fog has set in by the time I have made the turn onto MLK Drive. I round the corner to the wide spot in the road where the asphalt just disappears into the lake on my side, and I see the shapes. They are on the far bank. They move like mist, but somehow still beckon. Mallard Lake is shallow.

My car does not fully submerge.

I escape and feel the reeds brush my ankles. Then I feel reeds twist around my legs. The reeds grow fingers. The mist surrounds me. The water is shallow, but I can't escape.

RENOVATIONS: PART THREE (CRACK THE SKY) BY GARY MCDONOUGH

Ear piercing shrieks rang through the house. Shielding his ears with cupped hands, this made little difference, seemingly the horrific noise actually intensified. The skull increasing its efforts to penetrate his brain.

Driving Reece insane.

Feeling like his head would explode, he grabbed a tea towel and shrouded the skull, scooping it up he made his way outside into the cool night air. Outside was quiet, a stillness that contrasted with the farmhouse. Hurling the skull into the moat surrounding his home instantly halting the relentless screeching.

Upon his return, he welcomed the warmth of his bed, satisfied his ordeal was over. Lulled briefly into a sense of security; the bed began to shake as the house trembled from the very foundations. Sky rumblings like he'd never heard before, leaping from his bed he threw open the curtains in time to see the sky crack open. Lightning split the night sky, illuminating the entire area, causing the window to implode. Glass shower. Heavy downpours blowing through the recent void to his room.

A makeshift barricade would suffice till morning. The wind howled and rain fell as the storm continued to berate the house, Reece rested in the spare room, he knew the skull was responsible somehow. Sleep took him, hoping his house defied the storm.

Songbirds woke Reece, sun crept past the curtains warming his face. Stretching as he made his way to collect milk from the doorstep only there was more than a pint sitting on the mat.

BELATED WARNING BY MARINA SCHNIERER

An eerie feeling arose from walking into my Mother's new home, prickling the back of my neck. After a nasty breakup ending with threats, she walked away from her abusive partner.

No notable history was given about the house, however, its sadness was palpable. Aesthetically pleasing, yet there was no escaping the heavy feeling of depression lining its walls. Mother said I was wrong to feel that way but I was always 'spiritually sensitive'.

Unpacking the living room, an intense feeling overcame me. Horrifying visions I couldn't escape. Blood-spattered walls, pieces of flesh stuccoed to the furniture, a fleeting view of hacked up bodies lying lifelessly on the ground.

My trance was suddenly broken by three loud knocks on the front door. Mother calling out from the basement.

As the front door creaked open, heavy footsteps sounded in the hallway. A man I immediately recognized stood facing my way, a machete hanging loosely in his hand.

Turning to run, I felt an odd, cold sensation at the back of my neck. Coming from the stairs, Mother stopped dead in her tracks as she looked down in horror.

Following her shocked gaze, disbelief hit me upon recognizing the headless body lying lifelessly on the ground, my bloodied head just a few meters away.

Anger at the realization that his threats were all too real. The heart-wrenching pointlessness of the house's 'warning', too belated to do anything about.

Mother's guttural sounds penetrating the walls, my sadness and regret joining her screams.

THE RIPEST FRUIT BY CHRIS BANNOR

They came to feast, and I let them. They saw the fruit of the tree, ripe and dripping, and I watched them tear into the flesh as its juice stained the front of their Sunday Best.

They had abandoned me long ago, called me a pariah, and damned my soul. It was different now, they said, as they took my money, my gifts. As they shared my sumptuous feasts.

They woke suddenly from illusion, blood-stained and bewildered, and realized there was no tree. No fruit. Only the fetid flesh of their patriarch, dead upon the stake where I left him.

TAINTED TREATS

BY MCKENZIE RICHARDSON

Perched atop toadstools, the faeries picnic on fresh ticks. Though the wriggling delicacies usually feast on sweet hummingbird blood, these are filled with an odd-smelling liquid. They pop like blisters in their mouths, sending spurts of gelatinous crimson down tiny throats.

The blood incites strange cravings for ravens' feathers and slick slug slime, bone marrow, and cobwebs.

Yet no matter how much they eat, their stomachs still hunger for more.

Greedily fighting over a cicada's eye, two faeries snap vicious pointed teeth.

Others joined the melee until all sit munching mouthfuls, enjoying the papery crunch of each other's still-twitching wings.

SEE YOU IN HELL BY JENNIFER HATFIELD

Approaching someone as a spirit is easy. Hurting them, however, takes hard work and patience for the spirit. I can attest to that. I trained diligently for years to have enough ability to interact amongst the living. Just moving dust across the table takes a lot of practice and uses up a lot of energy. The longer it took me to accomplish my goal, the angrier I got.

"If I don't hurry and get this right, he's going to be dead before I can get to him."

Darren was HIV positive, a mere carrier. When he passed it to me, I suffered for months with illness, medications that didn't work, and starvation.

Tonight, I'm back for revenge.

I stood by him to watch him sleep. Until I began plunging the knife into him; stabbed his stomach, hit a lung, and who knows what else.

"There you son of a bitch, now you can suffer and feel pain."

He struggled to get up, reaching for the bedpost, only to have his fingers slip while his knife wounds slowly bled. I saw his eyes when he realized he wasn't leaving that room alive. He screamed until I punctured his throat with my knife.

"Should I stab his heart and stop his pain?"

Hearing the gurgling sounds, while I watched the blood pooling around him was satisfying. I dropped the knife, tip down, into his groin.

Then I whispered, "See you in Hell. We're both going there now."

CAMPING GONE WRONG BY ALANNA ROBERTSON-WEBB

How do you explain the sight of a creature like a bigfoot battling a creature like a wendigo?

You can't.

I quickly discovered that, even if you do try to, no one believes you. They called me a crazy liar, among other rude things, but I swear that's what happened to me last night.

I was camping by the shore of Lake Champlain, and an unholy chorus of growls and wails ripped me from slumber. I don't know which monster won, since all I could see was a tumbling heap of fur, blood, antlers, and flashing fangs as the two creatures engaged in a crocodile-like death roll.

Trees came crashing down, the embers of my dying fire were scattered and, as for me, I ran. I ran faster than I believed I could, faster than any P.E. teacher had ever clocked me at, and I didn't look back.

I wouldn't stop running, not even when my fear-leadened, sleep-addled mind realized that I had left my little sister behind.

God help me, I let her get torn to shreds by creatures that shouldn't exist.

DARK IN HERE BY L. ZEDDA SAMPSON

Stainless-steel presses cold and unforgiving against my back. It's dark in here; not even a pin-prick. And it's so cold. My body feels numb, but the panic grabs at my chest and radiates in waves with nowhere for it to go.

"*Let me out,*" I yell.

Doors open and close around me, muffled voices filter through the walls and cut in and out like a radio off-station.

A door flings open and light pours in. My body is rolled out. Someone else is rolled out too. Everything is light. Spectral shapes move around us like white shadows, prodding, listening, checking for life.

But I look only at the pale girl.

She's young, like me, about twenty-five, a similar build and colouring. Long hair matted black with blood frames deep gashes on her ruined face. There are more lacerations on her ribcage; her right breast is torn off. A wild animal scent lingers in the air. Compared to hers, my body is unblemished, my skin unmarked.

Our gazes lock, then the pale lady blinks.

The spectres come between us. "We've got a live one," one spectre says.

The hospital bed wheels away.

"What about me?" I say to the now-empty room.

A FRIEND FOR ELLIE BY P.J. BLAKEY-NOVIS

I only got the Ouija board out when I'd had a few drinks. I'd used it twice without result. The third time's the charm, so they say.

Now, my precious daughter, Ellie, is no longer lonely. She has a best friend who is always with her, or *within* her may be more accurate. I can't say I like the way she/they look at me sometimes, the unblinking stares and crooked grin, especially when I wake to find Ellie standing over me.

My daughter wouldn't hurt me. I'm not so sure about her friend, but at least she isn't lonely now.

THE STEAL BY CHRISTOPHER T. DABROWSKI

I died, but my soul, instead of going to the afterlife for a well-deserved rest, was still stuck on Earth. Moreover, it was divided into hundreds, if not thousands of parts.

It was trapped in shards of broken mirrors in which I looked at home, at my friends, at hotels and shops. Immobilized pieces of the soul enchanted for eternity on films, photographs, traditional and digital ones.

I was also crushed into car and bus mirrors, tram, or shop windows.

There is no heaven. The Indians were right: everything in which we are reflected steals our soul –piece by piece.

TIKO, IN A BOTTLE BY DANIEL R.

Being an immortal and purely instinct-driven creature, Tiko had no need of anything as mundane as *time,* so it had no idea of the vastness passed since its imprisonment. So long in fact that the continents only had rivers between them at the time.

Robbed of a corporal form that took centuries to construct, Tiko had been reduced to its base "spirit" form, and cruelly cast into a containment vessel made by filthy human hands.

A ghost of its former self, Tiko made use of photographic memory and studied from its mistakes. For centuries that turned into millennia that turned into eons, it played over and over again how it was defeated. Its conclusion? Simple arrogance. And luck. At some point, some feces ridden human had caught lightning with its hands and used it against the King of all creatures.

Humans, as a physical construct, were as weak as blades of grass and had been left unchecked by the other natural rulers. With no one to challenge the creature, it made frivolity of them. It kept them as pets and workers. Used them for its flesh crafting techniques and even mated with them. Weak of flesh they were, it discovered their *will* was stronger than iron-ore and coupled with its arrogance were able to deal a defeating blow.

Now, trapped deep underground, Tikos ghost listened to all things walk, crawl, and slither the world. It would be free again, one day. It was only a matter of....

GONE BY GABRIELLA BALCOM

Earthmaster Festus studied the charred remains of his home. So much work had gone into building it by hand, but it was beyond repair now. Gone. His beloved wife Ava had been singed in the fire, too, but at least she was alive.

Even though Firemaster Wardyl feigned ignorance, everyone knew he was to blame. Self-centered with a sense of entitlement, he liked getting his way, and Ava had rejected his advances.

He walked deep into the forest weeks later, hunting for wild game with bow and arrow. Without any warning, the consistency of the ground beneath him changed from solid to quicksand, and he dropped his weapons as he started sinking. He thrashed around in the thick ooze, looking frantically for something he could grab or use to pull himself out, but saw nothing. Breathing faster, he blasted his surroundings with fire but remained stuck.

"Help me!" he begged when Festus stepped from behind a cluster of oaks. "*Please!*"

The Earthmaster didn't respond, just leaned against a tree and watched silently.

Wardyl alternated between screams and pleas for help, the whole time sinking to his chest, shoulders, then his chin. He'd become hoarse by the time his head went under fully. Gurgles rang out, bubbles popping on the surface.

Snapping his fingers, Festus made the ground harden. No sign of quicksand remained now, and the Earthmaster walked away without a backward glance.

CATASTRO-PHEBY SERENA JAYNE

Shannon wrestled the Corgi-sized black cat from its carrier and dropped it on Aunt Janet's casket. "Steal her soul and I'll give you cream."

The cat scampered into the adjacent parlor and leaped onto the chest of the corpse on display.

Shannon's heart sank. "Bad Sith kitty."

She didn't know if kitty was fairy or demon, but she didn't pay to have the thing overnighted from Scotland to Chicago to ruin the wrong person's afterlife. "*Aunt Janet's* who disinherited me—not that *stiff*!"

With a flick of its tail, the beast darted past the stunned funeral director into the night.

IRIS IN THE FIELD BY JOHN IRVINE

One slender stem shivered in a chill dawn breeze, and Monty Granfield drew his wool scarf tighter around his neck. He stood, tense, glaring at the iris plant struggling to survive this early blast of freezing autumn weather. Although there was a bud on the stem, it was tightly closed and Monty hoped it would die.

Monty bent over the plant, cleared his throat, and spat a blob of thick, yellow mucous onto it. He smiled tightly, wiping his lips and savoring the moment.

"Bitch."

Two decomposing arms snaked from the ground, blackened fingers seizing Monty's ankles. Relentlessly, he was dragged feet first down into the soil. As the stinking dirt filled his mouth, Monty saw the bud open and the petals unfurl.

"Bitch."

THE OLD MAN BY AMBER M. SIMPSON

Vanessa watched as the old man walked by her house; thin, frail and limping.

"Hello," she said cheerfully. "Would you like a drink? Something to eat?"

Without a word, the old man came over. His bloodshot eyes were crusted; gray flesh sagged off his cheeks. His breath reeked of decay as he opened his mouth, long pointed teeth poking through purple-spotted gums.

Vanessa shrieked but couldn't run as his long pink tongue shot out like a frog's, and wound around her neck. Pulled into his hungry maw quick as a wink, the old man patted his engorged belly and burped.

VIDEO GAMES BY ELEANOR MERRY

"Power up, bitch!" Ryan yells as Shawn curses, tossing down his controller.

"Man, this is some bullshit, I'm going out for a smoke."

Ryan waves him off and goes back to the load screen, happy to play single player if his friend was going to be a whiney bitch about losing. The screen loads and Ryans' eyes widen as he sees a new option that didn't appear on the menu before.

"Full Immersion," he mumbles before shrugging and clicking **X**.

The screen fills with smoke and the sensation of dropping overwhelms him. Like a rollercoaster, his stomach flips and turns as he falls. It occurs to him that he feels like he's being pulled in all directions at once, but it isn't painful.

As his insides grow accustomed to the feeling, images begin to worm their way into his mind. Purple fog reveals endless zeros and ones, rolling past until they begin to weep red, a thick substance that grows and pours over the edge.

It all stops suddenly.

Ryan blinks a few times to get his bearings but he has to squint and the room is dark, a blinding light directly above him. Putting a hand up he looks up to the light and his heart drops in his chest when he looks up and sees his living room, Shawn coming back in from his smoke.

"Ryan?" His voice sounds distant and muffled.

"I'm in here!" He shouts back, but Shawn only shrugs and picks up a controller.

Around Ryan, the landscape changes. A man appears next to him, holographic and holding a gun. Ryan immediately recognizes it. Level seventy, the one he just completed.

He moves behind Shawn's character as the eggs around him begin to crack and small electronic spiders burst free. Suddenly, the character drops its ready stance and Ryan begins to panic. Looking up to the other side of the screen, he sees Shawn typing away on his phone.

He doesn't look up when Ryan screams as the

spiders overwhelm him.

CLASS NOTES
BY DAVID SIMMS

"Yes, Charlie?"

"The answer is Snow's Law of Thermodynamics."

Mr. Boggs sat back in his principal's chair, wondering how to trip up this precocious girl in his high school. "Where'd you learn that?"

The smile grew, even tilted on the pixie face framed by thin, chocolate hair. "You can't win, can't break even. Can't quit."

His face flushed. "You're not threatening me?" It was barely a question.

Charlie blinked. "No sir," she said, almost a purr. "It's Snow's Law."

Before that, he had quizzed her on Mozart's first instrument, the longest dynasty in Asia, and who wrote the first detective story. Nailed everything.

"Why are you in here?"

A soft shadow crossed her face. "Mrs. Leadbetter sent me to you. Suspected cheating."

"Did you?"

"You tell me."

The heady scent of something once rancid, now stale, with a tinge of spice wafted up to his eyes, causing them to water.

"You're also applying to graduate early."

A nod. "Yes sir."

Boggs gripped the transcripts. "What changed?"

She simply grinned. "I found I dug studying."

Which was her game? Phone? Watch? Hacking? His hands wavered.

"Can you empty your backpack for me?"

She upended it, the sounds of the bones rattling across his desk. "Grandpa told me you wouldn't understand. Necromancy isn't big around here. Plenty of cemeteries 'round here."

He recognized a phalange. It wore a familiar ring. "You know your mom misses singing you that song, don't you?"

She left with an offbeat rhythm beating through her bag.

THE PEOPLE UNDER THE ICE BY LANCE DALE

Bill pulled up to Stone Lake. There were no other cars. No other people. Perfect. He grabbed his fishing gear and waddled out onto the frozen surface. The guy at the bait shop warned him not to come here. Some nonsense about a curse and kids drowning. Bill didn't believe in that superstitious horse shit.

He drilled through the ice and set up his fish finder. It beeped whenever it detected a fish. He flipped the switch and it sounded like it was going to explode. He dropped his line through the hole, and something grabbed hold instantly. The force ripped the pole from his hands. He kicked his foot out to stop it from going in but slipped on the slick surface. He slammed face down. He saw their empty eyes staring back at him.

Children.

Their pale purple faces pressed up against the ice like a windowpane. They began hammering with their fists. Bill tried to climb to his feet but slipped again. An arm burst through and grabbed his leg. He kicked and struggled as more tiny arms punched through and clung to him.

Using all his strength, he jerked his body and rolled, breaking away from their grasp.

He was free.

A calmness filled the air. They were gone. No signs of the struggle were visible. Sunlight reflected off the ice's smooth glassy surface. *Did I imagine everything?* he thought and breathed a sigh of relief. It was muted by the sound of cracking beneath him.

NO-STRINGS-ATTACHED BY NATASHA SINCLAIR

Stalking, I watch the Manananggal as she shamelessly masquerades in human form through the shade of long days, until nightfall ceremoniously cloaks the land. Tearing herself in half, as the bat-like-wings burst through her bloodied back, I gag and swallow the rising, burning vomit at the sight of her self-evisceration. Grotesque entrails dangle, dripping blood like rain as she soars high into the night.

What she leaves behind —is mine until sunrise. Those legs wrap around my torso, and I plunder deep into her —there's definite life in the old girl. At least when detached —the best kind of no-strings-attached.

THE MAN IN THE CORNER BY LANCE DALE

"Mommy! Mommy! Come here!"

"What is it, sweetie?"

"There's a man in my room!"

"Sweetie, it was just a bad dream."

"No! He's real! He was right there. In the corner."

"Sweetie, there's nothing over there. Remember, I'm never going to let anything happen to you."

"You couldn't save dad from wrapping his car around that telephone pole and impaling himself on the steering wheel."

"What!?"

"His brains made the cracked windshield look like a stained-glass window."

"Stop it! Stop, right now!"

"Sorry, mommy. The man told me to tell you that."

"Where is this man!?"

"Standing right behind you."

AUNT AGATHA'S EXORCISM BY MIKE DEADY

"Father O'Malley, you have to come with me!"

"What's wrong, Ethan?"

"What? It's my Aunt Agatha. She just called and told me a demon is bothering her."

Father O'Malley grabbed his bible and a vial of holy water and got into Ethan's car. Moments later, they pulled up to Aunt Agatha's house. They rushed in and found her in bed. Father O'Malley splashed holy water on her and started praying.

Aunt Agatha woke up. "Ethan? What the hell is going on?"

"What? Father O'Malley is exorcising the demon."

"Ethan, you idiot! I told you I had edema, not a demon!"

MADELINE WORD COUNT BY DESTINY EVE PIFER

Darkness filled the room as the young girl lay motionless in bed. In the hallway, she could hear footsteps drawing near. She sank down in her pillow knowing that everyone else was asleep.

Slowly the door creaked open. "Madeline," a strange voice called out. The young girl peeked out from under the covers, but all she could see was darkness. She pulled the covers up to her neck and began to shiver.

"Madeline, come out wherever you are," said the voice which sounded much closer. Terrified she jumped out of bed but was quickly grabbed and pulled into the shadows.

IN THE VOICES OF THE OTHER ROOM

BY STEPHEN JOHNSON

The cries boom out like whispers at first
Searching for prey, an unending thirst
I cover my ears to block out the sound
To no avail, they are all around
In the Voices of the Other Room

A scratching claw across the wall
Footsteps disappearing down the hall

I shiver in my bed under the covers
Praying to be rid of the spirits who hover
In the Voices of the Other Room

Slowly I crawl from beneath the sheet
Dreading to discover what I should meet
Waiting for a hand from under my bed
To torture, grab and pull me dead
In the Voices of the Other Room

I walk slowly to the dark place
That scares me each night in this fearful space
Confident tonight I can face my fears
And finally, end my nights of tears
In the Voices of the Other Room

So Dear Reader I ask you one last request
If this be my final test
Remember to never listen to their cries
Or the unending lies
In the Voices of the Other Room

RENOVATIONS: PART FOUR (THE PRIEST) BY GARY MCDONOUGH

Blood vessels burst in the priest's bulging eyes as the noose tightened around his chubby neck, St Ambrose Barlow clawed at his new collar trying to gain purchase for that one last gasp of air as his body became a dead weight.

1641 was the year, having already been drawn; post hanging he was quartered and had his body parts boiled in oil after making the confession of being a Catholic Priest. The final defiant insult to his Catholicism was placing his severed, boiled head which was cover in blisters on a pike.

In the dead of night, a brave parishioner liberated the head from its resting place, providing sanctuary in his home, hidden in a hollow in a wall.

The latest update from Detective Crawley's team of researchers brought little comfort or support for Reece as the incessant screaming continued nightly. Nothing seemed to appease the head.

First, Reece treated it like a lord, resting it on soft cushions and talking to it before bed. Being nice changed nothing so Reece resorted to more destructive solutions. Hiding it in his barn, burying it in the ground, pounding it to dust, burning in the log fire may have brought Reece a moment of respite. The damned thing would return the next morning unscathed, sat on the doorstep ready for another turbulent night of unspeakable shrieking.

If Reece didn't get some sleep or help soon he might very well lose the plot. He was already imagining some pretty awful things.

WOLF MOON BY CHISTO HEALY

Darren stood in the middle of the dirt road, his eyes on the moon. It was full as can be, like a spotlight in the sky and he knew what it meant. She was coming. He hadn't known what she was when he took her. The thought now repulsed him, that he was inside an animal.

She had been beautiful, blonde, drunk. It was a mistake. Once you were started no meant yes. A howl sounded from somewhere. Darren was trembling. Paws padded from behind him. They were coming fast. He spun around to open jaws and screamed.

WOLF SPECTER BY SHANNON GRANT

At some points the creature would escape him, haunting the night by instinct. He didn't know what it did. All he knew was that it came back every night and entered his body, like a clockwork beast coming back to rest.

She watched him sleep, knowing one day she'd have to do something about the thing inside him. That beast was the reason she couldn't sleep at night. She would watch as the creature would rise up, out of him, to explore the earth.

She didn't know what he was capable of.

The creature was translucent, a wolf that rose and ran through the night. There were times she suspected it was a werewolf. She pondered whether or not it resided inside of him, or he had somehow created it.

One night she followed the creature outside. She kept out of sight as she watched it go into the woods, the specter trotting at first, then starting to run, freedom entering both its body and soul.

It found prey in a deer. She watched as it took the deer down, biting and gnawing at the flesh. The wolf specter somehow was eating.

She turned away. She couldn't handle it.

She woke the next morning and saw blood drying around his mouth.

It made her feel ill.

He had sworn to keep the secrets.

She hadn't.

The day after that, she watched as the villagers dragged him out of their cottage.

It made her feel safe.

A DIET QUITE UNIQUE BY MCKENZIE RICHARDSON

Martin had a parasite in his gut. Everyone does to a certain extent. Yet Martin's was unique.

A parasite feeds off its host and this one had a very particular diet. It didn't eat blood or tissue. It ate years.

At seventeen, Martin's hair turned gray. Skin wrinkled, bones went brittle. By twenty he'd aged a century. Still, the creature fed until Martin was nothing but dust, the parasite disappearing with his remains.

We all took the loss hard, no one more so than Martin's father. Poor man has aged at least five years in the days since Martin's death.

TIME FOR TEA BY SOPHIE WAGNER

"A tea party with me! Oh Darling, won't you join me for tea?" The thing sang, getting closer each minute.

Kylie dashed down the stairs and jumped towards the front door. Her hands stung as they hit the doorknob hard, but even more painful was the open and throbbing flesh wound on her back.

Tears streamed down her eyes as she turned the doorknob repeatedly, crying out in frustration as it refused to turn.

"A tea party with me! Oh, Darling, won't you join me for tea?" Sang the voice again. It sounded as if the singing was coming from the top of the stairs.

Hurriedly, Kylie ran through the kitchen and

stopped at the basement door. There was a cellar door that opened up into the yard from the basement. But the problem was, she could not remember if she had locked it.

There was hardly a moment to spare, the thing would find her whether she went downstairs or not. It was her last hope.

She dashed down the stairs, nearly tripping in her haste. Kylie sprinted with all her might towards the door, but quickly stepped back in fear when she saw a padlock holding it shut. Her stomach dropped, she had not put it there.

"A tea party with me! Oh, Darling, won't you join me for tea?" Kylie turned around to see the doll standing behind her. Its porcelain face was covered in blood and skin.

"Time for tea!" The doll lunged.

TO MARKET BY JOSH DARLING

Obsidian pillars marked the thoroughfare. A market for the denizen of hell to push their midnight voodoo wears. The creatures lined up, presenting their items on threadbare blankets to keep their merchandise off the ground.

A dozen baby's teeth for nightmares.

Cloth gold stars for oppression.

Vials of virgin menstrual blood for lust.

I've found what I'm looking for. The one tool to get it all. The way to take everything from the imps to the succubi who've lost their looks and now vend their possessions over their bodies. The demon pays me no attention as I load 6mm rounds into a Remington 700 bolt action rifle.

"That belonged to Charles Whitman," the thing selling it croaks.

Like I know who that is…

I figure there are enough bullets for me to kill them all, take all their stuff, and start up my own world domination plot.

I aim the gun at it, a perfect headshot…

He's an ugly thing, mostly long teeth, the kind for grabbing onto prey.

I can imagine its head exploding.

Now to make it happen, but instead, click.

The market is silent with excitement, the type of excitement found in the crowds at hangings or witch burnings.

It speaks, "Hey lady, that don't work with safety on, and we don't appreciate your kind here…"

"Easy fella, it just went off in my hands."

They can smell my lie and begin closing in on me.

THE PHONE CALL BY JODIE FRANCIS

"Am I speaking to Mr. Smith?"

"Yes, you are."

"This is Sheriff Houston; I hope you're sitting down. I have the most wonderful news for you. Your son has been found! He rang the station a few days ago, but of course we needed to verify it was him. I am so pleased to report that it *is* your son. He has been found alive! Everything checks out – we've done extensive testing. I can't even begin to imagine how you feel after twenty years…"

Mr. Smith put the phone down. Sheriff Houston was right, he couldn't imagine how he was feeling. His face turned white, his heart was racing, and his breath was coming in fast gasps. Mrs.

Smith was by his side.

"Is it true? What I just heard? Dear God, after all these years, it can't be true…" she wailed.

"It's just impossible," he breathed.

Ring, ring.

"Look I think we got cut off, let me pass you over to your son."

"Hello, Dad."

Silence spread through the call like a sickness.

"I told you that you wouldn't get rid of me that easily."

"It's just impossible, impossible," he kept repeating.

He looked to the backyard and the rose bush they planted over their son's body all those years ago.

"Impossible…."

BRING OUT YOUR DEAD BY VICTORY WITHERKEIGH

They are doing it again... trying to make my plague more complicated than they need to be.

I have never understood the need to question why things happen. It always seemed like such a stupid question. Does having a reason for dying to make the process any less painful? Less agonizing? When my legions infect and infest, destroying each cell bit by bit, does having a reason make it any better?

Death tells me he's witnessed enough of humanity's foibles to know that the reasons bring levity to the madness.

Seek and Destroy - that's what I do.

I devour within.

A PRICE TO PAY
BY N.M. BROWN

Six years ago, my wife Ava was taken from me. I wasn't feeling well and she went to the natural food market to get me some tea. Ava always made tea when I was sick, pampering me lovingly. She was walking down one of the aisles and had an aneurysm. She dropped dead right there in the spices section, her life snuffed out like a candle.

Food held no taste, water quenched no thirst and sleep gave no rest, not without Ava. I prayed to Heaven and to Hell for a solution. After days of searching, I finally found something.

The items are collected; the ritual performed. I feel exhausted in every way one's spirit can be.

Halfway through the day, the front door opens. I descend the stairs to see Ava place a bag of groceries down on the counter. She kisses me, then proceeds to flit about the house like no years had passed.

That night, Ava's bones contort and her eyes freeze over. She clutches her heart and drops off the bed, rigid by the time she hits the ground. I faint, wake up and it's morning again. Ava is laying there on her side smiling at me, with no recollection of the night before.

It's been almost one year since this started, we wake up every day together and I go to bed a widower. I'm losing my mind. What's worse, her eyes are starting to look the same alive as they do when she's dead.

AN UNSUSPECTING SACRIFICE BY AMBER M. SIMPSON

Erin struggled against the ropes that bound her to the tree, her moans muffled by the gag in her mouth. Her head pounded with pain. She'd been taking the short cut through the woods, walking home from a friend's house, when she'd heard the cracking of twigs and was struck from behind.

Sobbing, she gasped when a tall human-like figure emerged from the trees, its eyes glowing a fiery red.

Erin whimpered and thrashed as the creature approached, dragging with it the stench of decay. Its dagger-like claws slashed through her flesh, her insides twinkling in the moonlight like stars.

JUST A TAD BY M. BETTERELLI

A blackish-green orb the size of a softball popped up from the murky swamp water and laid still on the surface.

"Come here...come on... you can do it." Julie cupped her hands as she lowered them down, breaking the ripples that moved towards her. Subtle waves of motion trailed the orb as it slowly glided in her direction.

"That's it...you got it...I'm not gonna hurt ya." The softball-sized object inserted itself into the cupping of fingers as her thumbs held it in place. The jelly-like ball squirmed in her grasp as she raised it to her eyes. Now fully out of the water, two dark round eyes were visible on each side of it. A long flat tail protruded from its backside twice the length of its body.

"You're gonna grow up big and strong like the

rest of them." Slowly lowering her hands back to the water, the giant tadpoles buoyancy floated it out of her palms.

Its tail began to carry it out into the middle of the swamp, as areas of bubbles around it reached the surface. Larger round objects rose from the depths with glowing green eyes to greet it. "My how your family has grown." the girl said admiring them. Reaching behind her she felt for the handle of her bucket. The hodgepodge of body parts it contained fell with a splash as Julie heaved them out.. All green eyes seen, sunk quietly back into the swamp.

THE MARIONETTE BY MELODY E. MCINTYRE

"What an ugly, creepy marionette," I said to Suzanne, the thrift shop employee. It had a white painted face with red lips and black eyes that seemed to track my every movement. I shuddered and left, trying to forget the marionette.

My whole walk home I felt eyes on me like a spider on my neck. I quickened my pace until I was almost running. All I wanted was the sanctuary of my home, but when I finally opened my apartment door, the marionette was waiting for me on my kitchen table.

Panicked, I tried to call Suzanne at the thrift shop, but they were closed. I knew I would never be able to sleep with that thing in my house. Intending to throw it off my balcony, I picked up the marionette.

When my hands touched the marionette, its mouth fell open and a green mist poured out. The mist wound itself around my body starting with my feet. I started for the door but with each step, my limbs grew sluggish and stiff. Soon I couldn't move at all. I thought the apartment was growing larger, then I realized I was shrinking. By the time the mist had completely swallowed me, I was the same size as the doll. Everything faded to black.

The next day when Suzanne opened up the shop, she found two marionettes waiting on the shelf.

NOT ALONE BY CHISTO HEALY

Cecilia shivered. "Is anyone there? Can you hear me?"

She heard nothing but the crackle of static and the whistle of the wind. But the window was closed. Biting her lip she checked the readings on her EVP. Nothing.

Sighing, she thought maybe she wasn't cut out for ghost hunting. She was sure this place was haunted. "Is someone here? Can you hear me? Please speak. Are you here?"

"No," a voice whispered into her ear. She could swear that she could feel the lick of a tongue.

"What is your name?" She was afraid now.

Nothing.

"Are you still there? Where are you?"

"Here," said the phantom as he appeared before

her seizing her with his long-dead hands. She opened her mouth to scream but it was cut short as she was whisked away, pulled through a rift in the darkness, a doorway in the shadows. All that remained was the EVP reader that finally lit up and moved to signal that there was a presence in the room.

Cecilia continued to scream from where she was, to beg for help, and the dial on the EVP reader jumped back and forth. She was pounding at the barrier with her fists, staring into the empty room. The space between rippled like water when her knuckles connected with it. Her pounding created a breeze that blew through the room despite the closed window.

Behind her laughter sounded.

SHE STARES BACK BY TARA LOSACANO

She opens her eyes to darkness. She feels it in the room with her as she lays in her bed. It has been so long since it has visited, she thought it had finally left for good. A shiver runs down her spine as she feels the air turn brittle with cold. She doesn't want to look, knows she shouldn't. But finally, her eyes slowly turn toward the corner of her shadowed bedroom.

She shudders when it comes into view. The staring eyes are insidious and black. The gaping mouth hangs open in an eternal silent scream. She tries to speak, to ask it why it is here. But she is paralyzed in agonizing fear. For the dead, disturbed face that she stares back at is her own.

CURSED EARTH
BY RJ MELDRUM

The bulldozer rumbled into the field. The serenity of the place was destroyed in an instant. John, the driver, was there to clear the field of corn and to prepare it for the construction crews. He noticed a scarecrow, propped up against the fence.

"Sorry, bud. Your job is over."

He started the engine. A shadow fell over the cab. He glanced up and saw the scarecrow staring in at him.

This land is protected

The whisper came from the corn.

The cab door was opened. He was pulled out, screaming. After a few moments, the silence and serenity returned.

IT WAS JUST ANOTHER DAY AT WORK... BY RAINIE ZENITH

Helen Stilton lumbers out the door on screen and my jaw plummets in amazement. It was only yesterday she was admitted on a gurney, unmoving, unfeeling, grey-faced. She really shouldn't be leaving the building of her own accord.

It's my job to monitor the morgue's security footage, you see.

Before I can alert anybody, there's a knock at the security office door. As I move to open it, movement on another of the security screens catches my eye. It's James Ferris stalking through the west wing corridor. James was one of the morgue's top forensic pathologists.

He died a week ago.

My hand freezes on the door handle.

"Who's there?" I demand.

A rasping exhalation is the only response. I grab a chair and jam it beneath the handle as the knob begins to twist. I catch it just in time.

I look back to the screens and see movement throughout the building, people shuffling restlessly down the halls. Not people; *bodies.*

The doorknob twists again.

THE WISHING PIPE BY M. BETTERELLI

Craig grabbed the bong in his right hand and situated the bowl in his left. A reverberant voice came from within the glass cylinder along with shimmering green sparks.

"I am the Genie of the lamp! What are your three wishes?"

Craig looked at his water pipe puzzled. "Uh..it's a bong, bruh." He continued to pack the ground plant into its bowl.

The same voice came again. "Yes, I am the Genie of the...bong! Your wishes still remain thrice."

Craig reasonably said, "I wish for more weed man." Suddenly a plastic bag appeared on the table in front of him, plump with green nuggets.

"What is Masters second wish?" The Genie of the bong asked. Craig sat there calmly loading a bowl full of his new pungent treasure.

"I don't know man. I guess I wish for a soda." A drink appeared on the table in front of him, ice-cold to the touch.

The disembodied voice of the Genie called out again. "Master's third and last wish will be?"

In annoyance, Craig said the first thing that came to his mind.

"I wish you'd just let me smoke this bong man."

The Genie quieted, and his eyes widen in fear. Craig raised the cylinder to his lips while simultaneously lighting the bowl. He inhaled with such force, the Genie couldn't hold on from being sucked into Craig's chest. Eyes clenched tight from the absorption, two essences collided. Craig opened his eyes.

"I am now the Genie of the... Craig!"

UNDERWORLD GOD BY NATASHA SINCLAIR

A monsoon of shrieking screams flood the darkness, Batara Kala reveling in torture play. The stench of charred flesh and blood seeps from volcanic-like rock walls — just another day in his Underworld.

In the early days he'd break humans too easily; pitiful spirits and bodies too fragile, mangled quickly by the sadistic God — they'd shatter, crumbling pathetically like flimsy glass beneath his deadly grotesque palms.

Thousands of years have aided Batara Kala in honing his exquisite skill of suffering infliction. He is the king of the dammed's eternal torment.

Prejudice non-existent in his sordid kingdom.
Pain foisted generously upon all.

THE MERMAID AND THE FISHERMAN: A DARK FAIRY TALE BY JOSHUA E. BORGMANN

I found a mermaid in my nets, and she promised three wishes for a price.

I wished for the most beautiful wife and found her waiting for me.

Beauty called out for wealth, so I wished for unlimited wealth. I didn't care about the mermaid's tears or the countless dead fish that she clutched.

I found myself richer than Gates and turned a blind eye to the hurricane that leveled New Orleans.

Of the weeping mermaid, I demanded that my wife and I be made unique among all of humanity.

We were immune to the plague that soon killed everyone else.

FACELESS BY LEON SLUYTER

It was a horrendous but fantastic nightmare that occurred many times. The faceless woman would torment him and cover him with blankets to smother him. As he lost his will to fight, he´d give in to the temptation of eternal slumber.

At that moment, she pulled the blankets away to prolong his punishment, he´d wake with a scream clenched between his teeth.

He took a shower to wash away the feelings of lingering dread. He felt empowered when he opened the door to the attic.

It all came back to him now!

The face of that whore nailed to the wall, he spat her in the face and laughed.

"What are you going to do now, bitch?"

He almost succumbed to a heart attack, when he heard a familiar voice answer him.

"I'm going to kill you, but first I'll torment you. Now, turn around and face me!"

Slowly, he turned around, it was her. She had come to reclaim her face.

As she walked towards him, he began to wail in agony.

The decomposing woman touched his face and he knew he wouldn't wake screaming in his bed this time. Trembling with fear he pushed her away, but she appeared in front of him in a split second.

This was going to be a hell of a way to die....

JUDITH BY JOHN IRVINE

It's obvious when I find Judith sitting motionless in front of the mirror again this morning, grey hair hanging like greasy rats' tails about her pallid face, that she isn't going away. Her floral print dress barely contains the disgusting conglomeration of doughy flesh. A single tear slides down my cheek, more than she deserves.

It seems only yesterday she was her old self: overbearing, demanding, fat arse wobbling in unison with her screeching voice and waggling finger. I can almost hear her squawking in that off-key voice,

"Albert? Take out the garbage! And walk the dog, you lazy sumbitch! And don't be too long, Mother's comin' for dinner! Albert? Don't you go smokin' those foul cheroots out there and stinkin' up the house with your smelly clothes. And be nice to Mother, got me?"

I got her, all right, one week ago.

How I thank God for giving Man fine Sabatier edgeware and the strength to drive a long, sharp, carbon steel piece of it into the chair back, right through the miserable bitch's black heart…

"Albert!"

I face an unbelievable, I-must-be-freaking dreaming sight and stumble backward.

She's on her feet, wobbling only slightly, and through gas-bloated blue lips, she starts in on me again.

"Albert? What've you been up to? There's a terrible stench in here." A fragment of rancid flesh falls from her hand as she waggles a finger at me. *"If I didn't know better, I'd say somethin' died in here! Albert?"*

VESSEL BY JOHN CADY

As much as I wanted to, I couldn't look away from that mirror. Though I thankfully couldn't smell the burning flesh, the image alone of the flames making short work of what little clothing was there before moving onto the flesh was more than capable of haunting my dreams henceforth. I could handle it, however, if it meant he'd no longer be haunting our home.

The "he" I speak of was the house's previous owner – the one who perished in the fire. We thought only his ashes remained. We were wrong. His spirit needed a vessel to leave. I volunteered.

BLOOD ON THE GROUND BY GABRIELLA BALCOM

Humberto chanted, performing satanic rites, and killed a chicken while his followers watched. He drained its blood into a chalice, accidentally dribbled some on the ground, and felt vibrations underneath his feet.

"It's working," he announced. Grinning widely, he poured more blood onto the sediment where the first had landed.

But Humberto fled when the earth split open, forming a gaping maw that swallowed several Satanists.

Arms of dirt shot from the ground, tearing others apart, then merged, taking the shape of an enormous foot.

"*You will defile me no more,*" the earth boomed, and the foot stomped Humberto flat.

NOT SO EMPTY HOUSE
BY RADAR DEBOARD

The complete silence that filled the almost empty house was normal for Raul. After all, he lived alone in a remote house. Isolated from most, with the nearest town over fifty miles away.

He was alone, except for the figure draped in a white wedding dress, stained with splotches of red.

It followed him wherever he went in the house, constantly nipping at his heels. Each night, appearing above his head as he tried to sleep, the visage of his dear Isabelle looking down at him in anger. It seemed as though he would never escape the ghosts of his past.

BAD LUCK BY AMBER M. SIMPSON

The black cat darted across their path just as they rounded the corner.

Trina gasped. "That's bad luck!"

Derek rolled his eyes. Superstitions were dumb. To prove it, he chased the cat down the sidewalk, threading his way through a horde of pedestrians.

It stopped at the curb and sat on its haunches, tail twitching back and forth.

As Derek approached it, a fire escape ladder came loose above him, crushing and breaking his back. Horrified screams polluted the air while the black cat, purring, padded over. It licked the blood streaming from Derek's mouth with its rough, sandpaper tongue.

UPSKIRTING BY DAVID O. HUGHES

The massive corkboard in his den was covered in his unorthodox photos. A snap here, a click there, and Derek had amassed his Collage of Cunt: bald, bushy, young, old, vajazzled, tattooed, and a transvestite delight.

He now eyed the purple-haired punk who stood with her back to him.

My first *rocker*! he thought.

Derek moved closer, bent, and placed his camera under her skirt.

She squatted, catching him off guard.

"You're *fucked*, perv!"

Green liquid squirted down her thighs, drenching his arm to the elbow. The corrosive fluid chewed through his flesh, causing it to snap, sizzle and pop.

THE PACT BY CHRIS BANNOR

The pact was made, and the spirit writhed over his flesh. It burrowed under his skin like a worm digging through fresh-tilled earth. His breath stilled but his heart raced, making him feel that time had stopped and sped up.

His legs buckled, and he landed on his knees. The spirit paid his pain no mind, and he threw his head back, screaming his consent to the night sky.

The loa came for his need of vengeance tonight, and he'd given his body. The pact etched its way onto his bones, and only blood would satisfy the god's newfound thirst.

HUNTER IN THE FOREST BY MCKENZIE RICHARDSON

The tightening in his gut forced his mind to surface through the blackness. His vision filled with a woman's sneering face, cracked and knotted like ancient wood.

The anger in her eyes sent a rush of memories flooding back; notching his arrow, watching it fly, its point piercing the deer's side. He should've known better than to trespass in these woods.

Emerald energy crackled as the woman raised her hand, gnarled fingers extended.

The pain in his stomach migrated upward through his chest, his throat. He opened his mouth to scream, but only vines emerged, blood-soaked thorns dappled with flesh.

CURSERBY SERENA JAYNE

Curser was the perfect name for the blasted thing. It's blinking burrowed into Hannah's head, invading her dreams, and stealing every spare second.

It beat like a heart. Something alive. Something undead.

Into a fugue state, she'd slide, losing time as well as smidgens of her sanity. The curser drew her in, becoming a gateway for the novel from hell to drag her in. Leach-like, the document drained her energy and spirit. She'd add words to the page, delete some, add more. The never-ending hamster wheel of revision.

"Bestseller," the ghost in the machine whispered.

Hannah believed it's pretty lie.

RENOVATIONS: PART FIVE (THE BARN) BY GARY MCDONOUGH

Less than a week after his previous visit, Detective Crawley returned to the farm with what he thought was would be welcomed news. Finally, some advice that may silence the skull. Rapping his knuckles on the old Oak door, eager to share his possible solution. There was no answer, so he knocked again. Still no reply; he tried the handle, it opened…

"Mr. Cottam, it's Detective Crawley, may I come in? I have some useful information I wish to share!"

The detective noticed the skull resting on a velvet cushion on the kitchen table. Crawley felt like he was being watched, how could an inanimate object be eyeballing him? He shouted once more before leaving a note for Reece to contact him as soon as possible. An ominous feeling grew heavy on the detective the longer he stood in the kitchen.

Stepping outside brought relief. He noticed the barn door blowing open and shut as he was about to leave. An icy chill ran the length of his spine as he went to investigate if Reece's car was still home.

Reece's car was home as was Reece. He was hanging from the center rafter of the barn, finally at peace.

All Crawley could think was that if he had called a day sooner, the solution may have saved Reece's life.

After the funeral, the wall which Reece demolished was restored; the skull placed back where it was discovered. Silently sitting there to this day.

SKIN STRIPS BY NATASHA SINCLAIR

Fae circling, they stalk—teeth gnash-grinding, chitter-chattering.

Crisp crunch snaps conceal anticipation squeals.

Ghost tales shared, shivering and laughing scared.

Mummy-bags beckon friends to slumber.

Fire snuffed, fastened down, zipped in.

Rustling bags give way to sleep, none restless counting sheep.

The hooting, scuttling nightlife submit to silence as swarming, hungry hunting Sith flutter and creep.

Claws tear through everything but sleep.

Razor black talons slice dermis.

Thin strips, all layers plundered — complete skin deep.

Stripping to exposed raw muscle.

Forked tongues lapping pools of metallic-sweet nectar blood.

These wildling's saliva — toxic, paralytic salt.

Victims wake — not one can scream.

PALE AS THE MOON BY GEMMA PAUL

She stepped off the train, the epitome of sophistication and grace with her long black corseted dress that pulled her ample bosom up high, her porcelain feet encased in black stilettos, and the black jeweled cloak tied around her neck with a collar reaching up high. A Victorian lady of the night with a beauty to rival any.

Raven steps off the train onto the dusty ground of the little backwater railroad town she has traveled to in the dead of night. She watches as a ball of tumbleweed rolls right by her feet in the gentle night breeze.

"Charming," she says as she looks at the town void of nightlife.

She lifts one finger to regally wipe at the corner

of her mouth. A smear of blood transfers to her finger, she looks down at the red stain before placing the finger in between her luscious red lips and sucks.

The train chugs off, steam billowing out of its pipe as it heads into the dead of night, screams echoing from inside out into the desolate landscape. Raven smiles at the noise as she steps away from the railway tracks and towards the only building lit from within, the Saloon.

Inside the train, a woman stands at the entrance to one cabin, screaming at the top of her lungs as she takes in the sight before her. Twenty people lie dead, slumped throughout, as pale as the moon, their blood drained from their bodies.

ANGEL BITE BY TINA SWAIN

Sunsets were her favorite. It knew this as she unknowingly absorbed her last one.

At dusk, her body was mauled beyond recognition, feathers and reticulated tendon.

Each one knew the secrets, sins, and desires of their coveted.

Perched above the dripping streets, they wept aloud in contrition preening the blood from their wings. Judgment had begun. The night's shadows kept voiceless secrets as the guardians turned on their flock in unison. The most exquisite creatures with inklike eyes never seen nor heard, cast from heaven to deliver hell on earth one mortal at a time. The sentinel would now partake.

THE SWITCH BY J. EDWIN BUJA

The reflection in the mirror startled Glynnis. The hairy face, the snout, the pointed ears atop her head. The only thing that hadn't changed was the green of her eyes.

Could this really be happening?

She tore open her robe to scratch at the terrible itching on her chest.

No! Eight breasts! She felt ridiculous.

More hair everywhere. Muscular arms and legs that ended in paws. A tail?

Impossible!

The wind blew the bathroom curtain aside to reveal a full moon.

A month ago, she and her darling Rex had been out for an evening walk in the woods. Rex had stopped dead, growling at something stalking them. A blur rushed from the bushes, swatting her brave Rex out of the way as he tried to protect her. Her best friend dead.

The thing had bitten her.

Glynnis howled at the moon.

There was a crash at the back door followed by heavy footsteps heading in her direction. Her ears twitched. The bathroom door flew open to reveal...

The most handsome man she had ever seen. He stood silently, naked, fully aroused.

Impressively aroused.

The man looked a little confused then smiled at her. Taking tentative steps towards her, he held out a hand as if to say hello.

Something primal from deep within made Glynnis want to rip his throat out.

Then she saw what was around his neck.

A collar with the word REX.

She growled and tried to smile. Maybe things wouldn't be so different after all.

DANCE BY MIRIAM H. HARRISON

He only saw them dance when the raindrops fell. He could hear their footfalls among the patterings of rain as they danced between the drops. They moved like a mist, furling and unfurling beneath the moonlight, their mesmeric undulations filling the empty spaces. He crept through the trees and shadows to watch—alone, but not unseen.

She was fresh as the rain, ancient as the rain, timeless as the rain. She breathed the lost souls into the night, spun them amid the falling drops. They drew him in, step by dancing step, but she would be the one to draw him out—out of his mortal vessel and into their endless dance.

CAKE BY RUTHANN JAGGE

Every October, he had a special cake made to celebrate their time together. She would always be beautiful to him, and he promised to love her forever.

This year's cake was decorated with thick icing in shades of pink, her favorite color, detailed with loopy sugar-bows and perfect edible roses. The vivid accents reminded him of her lipstick. He missed her kisses terribly.

He knelt and carefully slid the confection from the cardboard box, placing it gently near a granite headstone along with a single red rose.

"Enjoy, my Sweetheart, I think this is the nicest one yet, hope you'll like it too." The air around him grew cold as he walked away folding the box under his arm.

"Thank you, my love," she whispered. He heard loud chewing and contented sighs as her sticky black fingernails dug deep into the delicious layers. He quickly left the cemetery without looking back.

She would be satisfied for another year.

THIS ISN'T VERY EXCITING BY RAINIE ZENITH

Joey wanted to hang out in the local cemetery on Halloween night, so I tagged along. I don't believe in ghosts or anything, so there wasn't really anything to be afraid of, was there?

We sat in the dark on a marble grave, drinking cans of bourbon.

It was me that broke the silence.

"This isn't very exciting," I said.

The stone lid beneath us rattled.

"What the hell?" Joey said.

I sprang up.

It rattled again.

Joey and I backed away and watched in awe-struck terror as the heavy lid grated aside, releasing a smell of decay like day-old roadkill.

It wasn't the kind of excitement I had wanted.

A skeletal hand emerged, followed by an empty-socketed skull draped with hanging flesh, a rotting corpse stepping from the grave like something out of a nightmare.

We fled.

Later, Joey blamed it on the alcohol.

Me? I will no longer set foot in a cemetery.

FORMULA
BY MASON H. HILDEN

"Oh, dear God, she's going to finish the second bottle! We need more formula! Hurry, Steven!"

Steven bolts from the baby's room and scrambles down the stairs to the kitchen. He viciously opens the fridge, panic setting in as he is unable to locate the formula.

"I can't fuckin' find—"

"Top shelf, behind—"

"Got it! Hold on baby, I'm coming!" Steven is halfway up the stairs when he hears a blood-curdling scream from Tammy.

Steven enters the room and immediately cries out as he bears witness to the carnage. He drops the bottle, it landing beside a blood-splattered stuffed animal.

Sprays of crimson decorate the room, and standing over the body of his wife is a tiny creature, its teeth, and claws covered in blood and gore. Two empty baby bottles are at their feet.

The abomination that was – that is – their daughter, turns toward her *daddy* with her innocent eyes, smiles, and says, "Baba?"

DRACHMAS
BY B.F. VEGA

Uncle Walter had found the coins when he was on his first archeological expedition to Greece. I think he stole them from a grave. As his executor, I was to put one on each eye and then make sure the coffin was securely shut.

I fully intended to follow Uncle Walter's orders. I don't know what came over me. Right before they closed the coffin, I swapped the drachmas for quarters. Immediately after the first shovelful of dirt was thrown in the hole, I looked up to see Uncle Walter glaring at me. He was there one second and gone the next. I shook my head and went to get into the car to go to the funeral reception. The hearse somehow came out of gear and struck me. I was in the hospital for a month.

Leaving the hospital, I saw Uncle Walter again. I tried to point him out to the nurse, but she had run back inside for something. The brakes on the wheelchair chose that moment to fail.

I never saw the ambulance that hit me. The next thing I knew I was on a misty riverbank with Uncle Walter and an angry man in a toga. I don't know how long we were fighting over the coins before they disappeared from view.

My girlfriend was supposed to bury me with the drachmas. I can't wait until that traitor gets here.

THE GAME BY MELODY E. MCINTYRE

Rob showed Sarah the mysterious video game he'd found at the flea market. The cover proclaimed that it was haunted. Playing along correctly would summon benevolent spirits that would bring great wealth upon the players, but if they failed, then dark twin spirits would steal their breath away. The cover advised caution, but to Rob and Sarah, two horror buffs, it sounded like the perfect cheesy date night.

Sarah set her laptop up in the living room and hunted down her old DVD drive. They couldn't remember the last time they'd played a game with an actual CD. Rob turned down the lights as Sarah fired up the game. Red letters scratched their way across the screen announcing that if they followed the instructions exactly, no harm would befall them that night.

The temperature dropped as they played, but when Sarah checked the thermostat, it insisted she was mistaken. Rob could feel eyes all around him, but the two of them were alone. Swallowing their fears, the couple played on.

When they were asked to draw eerie symbols in red ink, they obeyed and in unison, they recited the incantations that flashed across the screen. After an hour, the game ended and they laughed in relief when the credits reminded them the game was for 'entertainment purposes' only.

They kept laughing until a set of icy fingers closed around each of their throats.

THE MARBLED STALKER BY MAGGIE D BRACE

As Grammy slowly succumbed to dementia, we used our fleeting time left with her gathered around her bedside regaling each other with re-membered joy and tender moments. My brother, ever macabre, retold family lore of Grammy's beloved, angelic younger brother who died mys-teriously in his sleep while some evil presence fiendishly dropped marbles down the wooden stairs to scare and confound his family. That was eighty years ago, now she lay in an unconscious state.

That night, I was awakened by an inexorably horrific feeling. A hideous sense of darkness overwhelmed me. I lay sweating and shaking in my bed, unwilling, unable to get up and check on my grandmother. I heard a muffled plop, then another one.

Summoning all my courage, I threw back the quilt, crept across my room on tiptoe, and peered into her darkened bedside. The sight before me made my stomach roil and a shiver coursed down my spine. A greyish vapor was encircling her. Slowly, it began to manifest itself into a curious four-legged mongrel, perched atop her chest.

A snarling voice rent the air and shiny marbles plopped out of the beast's maw as it rasped, "*I've sought ye long, Josephine. Ye be mine now!*" It sensed my presence and turned to pounce on me, but Grammy grabbed it by its scruff and howled.

The shadowy form dissipated as I approached. Grammy was lifeless but had a beaming smile on her face. She had won her final battle.

ALL IN THE FAMILY BY NICOLE HENNING

"I'll be fine, Mom; I've just had a lot of nightmares lately."

Macey rubbed her eyes wearily as she fought the urge to throw her cell phone across the room.

"I keep seeing a man's face and…never mind… Ok, I love you too. See you tomorrow. Bye."

Tapping the end call button she decided to try to go to bed while she was tired and gave up on doing anything else for the night. She silently cursed herself for moving into her deceased Uncle's old apartment.

Once she was snuggled in her pile of blankets she fell asleep instantly, only to wake up two hours later with a scream bubbling in her throat. Throwing her blankets off of her she struggled to not fall as she got out of bed and ran for the light switch. She couldn't stop herself from uttering a cry when the light switch failed to make any light. She stood with her back to her bed panting and tried to calm herself and froze when she heard feet walking across the carpet behind her. They weren't rushing but held no hesitation in their gait.

Macey staggered back towards the bed and grabbed for her phone on the nightstand. The next night her mother sank to her knees next to the bed screaming in terror. Macey's body was stretched half off the bed, her mouth open in fear. Her phone, almost dead, showing the picture of her Uncle reaching for her.

FURY BY GABRIELLA BALCOM

Obsessing about his ex-wife Viola's upcoming marriage, Lemuel remembered her infidelity and fumed. He merged with the wind and sent gales swirling in all directions.

Rage and hatred intensifying as he swept across town, he blasted open Viola's door, finding her in her beau's arms. Lemuel raked them with jagged talons of air, ripped them to pieces, and didn't stop till they lay shredded on the floor.

Unsatisfied, he gusted one direction, then another, pulverized everything in his path, and ignored the blood flying through the air. He didn't stop until he'd leveled the city and body parts lay everywhere.

TERROR IN THE GRAVEYARD BY ANDREW KURTZ

The caretaker shone his flashlight on the tombstones in the cemetery before heading home.

Suddenly, a harsh voice broke the peacefulness of the night, "*I am getting out of this damn coffin and starving for human flesh!*"

Sweat began to pour down the caretaker's cheek as his hands started to tremble.

"Who's there?" he called out, hoping not to get a reply

"*I am over here and clawing my way out,*" came the response.

A river of yellow fluid poured down the caretaker's leg but he couldn't move, paralyzed with fear.

"Please, stay in your grave!" he cried out.

"*I am covered in maggots and my skin is rotting and putrid. I hunger to feast on the living,*" the voice informed him.

Feeling light-headed, he shone the flashlight on the graves once more, searching for the origin of the voice.

"Please don't do that. You're dead," the caretaker pleaded as his heart rapidly beat.

"*I can feel the night air on my rotting bones. You are in my sights!*" the voice screamed.

The caretaker clenched his chest and his breathing became heavy.

"Stay in your coffin," he meekly whispered, as he collapsed on the ground.

"*I am coming for you now and will rip your flesh apart!*

"No! Leave me…." The caretaker did not finish his sentence, his heart finally stopping, the fear too much to bear.

The flashlight rolled out of his hand and onto the grass before laughing. "*What's the matter? You can't take a joke?*"

EMILY'S DOOR BY STEPHEN JOHNSON

The worn doll stared out from behind the other trinkets on the shelf. Strands of yellow frayed hair dripped down covering its eyes. Several people walked by never noticing the hand-made doll until a young man pulled her to freedom. "Emily will love you," he whispered as he grabbed the treasure.

Jason surprised Emily in the kitchen.

"Happy birthday!" She shrieked as he produced the doll from behind his back.

"It's perfect!" She raced upstairs to her doll collection to admire her new addition. She marveled at the design as she pulled strands of hair from its face to reveal two dark eyes. Her smile faded as she was pulled into another place. Cold and damp, all she could see was darkness. Panic overtook her as she sensed the burning black eyes of the doll. Only a door stood in the darkness and she ran towards it grabbing the handle and pulling.

*　*　*

Jason checked into the psychiatric wing and took the familiar path traveled over the last six months. He sighed as he noticed Emily in the same spot staring absently at the wall.

"I brought you something you might like." He set the doll into her folded hands, "I found her in your room. Now, she can always look over you."

Emily jerked on the door as she listened to his distant voice but crumpled to the ground as she heard the other familiar voice gutturally whisper, "You can never leave me. Stay with me forever."

UNDEAD BY JOHN IRVINE

Undead? I hate the word. Pure Hollywood *chic*. Undead? It's an oxymoron at best, uninformed at worst. I'm walking around. I eat. Is that undead? Do you eat and walk around? You do? Are you *un*dead? No, I thought not. See what I mean?

Hey... do I knock gays and transvestites? Blacks? Jews? Canadians? I don't draw welfare. I don't drive a petrol-guzzling car. I don't drink or smoke. I like to think of myself as enhanced. Augmented. Ameliorated.

So, I eat people. But I don't eat dead people. That's a rumor. Or junkies. And I refuse to eat politicians... I'm fussy. I don't like the taste of shit. Haha. A little grave humor there. OK, so you're not amused.

I can't die. Forget about it. I'm immortal. As long as I eat people I'm OK. If I run out of people

I'm in trouble. I can't see that happening, can you? I thought not.

You're a Christian? Well, well. Isn't that curious? Ate a Muslim once. Touch on the bitter side, I thought. Took a lot of unwrapping. Your god made everything, right? Including me? Ah... I'm an abomination now, am I? Spawn of Satan. That's your typical Christian dogma for you. What else should I expect?

Anyway, can't chat any longer. Places to go. People to eat. *Bon appetit.*

LONG WAY HOME BY JACEK WILKOS

I finished my work very late today and there was a long way home before me. I left the city lights behind and sank into the blackness of the night, lit only by the headlights of my old Ford.

Driving along the empty road running through the fields, I noticed a silhouette on the side of the road. I wouldn't have the heart to leave anyone in the middle of nowhere, so I stopped and offered a ride. I had a lot of stuff on the front seat, so the stranger sat in the back.

A few minutes later, we came across a road accident. Flashing red and blue lights illuminated the darkness of the night. As I passed the traffic policeman, I turned my head and saw paramedics zipping up a body bag. I saw the face of the deceased for a brief moment.

A face, strangely familiar.

When I realized where I saw it before, I trembled with fear. I slowly looked up to the rearview mirror.

THE NIGHT BEFORE BY CHISTO HEALY

Miranda slept. It wasn't her usual sleep. It was something deeper. She saw things but it wasn't a dream. It was a connection, a bond forming, tying her to the one who did this. She could see her, feel her, not just on her flesh but inside her, warming her. It was sensual, beautiful.

The goblet was still by her bedside, where Miranda had drunk of her. The stain remained like lipstick as she slept. When she awoke, when the time came and the ritual was complete, she would be different, better, eternal like her master.

CANNONBALLS AND MUSKET FLASHES: LIMITED EDITION BY DAVID O HUGHES

"Can we play my new board game?" William asked.

"Yes," Dad said.

"Green army!" Mum claimed.

After forty minutes of play, the dice displayed

six sixes...

Roll the magic numbers, William thought, cowering behind the sofa. A war raged between red, black and green coats.

And bring the action into *your home....*

A heavy stench of cordite hung in the air, as dragoons and infantry slaughtered one another.

William poked his head up and spotted his father entangled in barbed wire, and his mother lay close by, a bayonet buried in her chest.

A trooper charged his way, his saber drawn....

THE OTHER ME BY P.J. BLAKEY-NOVIS

It is difficult to describe what it looks like, always in the periphery of my vision. Occasionally, I catch a glimpse of the white eyes, the blackened teeth. If I try to focus on it, then it disappears. Paranoia personified. Following me. Always close, yet out of reach.

It is dangerous, claiming victims wherever I go, leaving them for me to find. I'm always the one who finds the bodies; they are my hands which turn crimson under the moonlight.

One day it will take me too, but only when it is ready. For now, I wait, avoiding the shadows.

UNHONORED
BY CHRIS
BANNOR

As she walked the new road home, she heard a child's cry. The cry became a wail, though, and she covered her ears to block it out.

She stumbled as something jumped onto her back. Her hands and knees were bloodied when she fell, but the wail continued unabated. Now, she heard words behind the torment, though.

Give me peace.

She couldn't stand, confused and crazed from the cry of the Myling at her back. The creature bellowed in rage, and the last thing she felt was the dig of hands in her flesh and the sting of biting teeth.

JACK BY SURINA VENKAT

Everyone in the house loves Jack. How could they not? He's a golden bundle of joy that always has a smile on his face and wet kisses at the ready when you're feeling down. And when he's in a room, the entire place seems to brighten, like even the house adores him. He's perfect.

When he dies, he's surrounded by the children. Marcie sniffs and Elliot cries and my heart sinks. Jack had been so little–I had thought he was safe.

How foolish of me to become so complacent.

"I'm going to miss him," Marcie says.

"Me too," I say. "I wish it had liked this one."

I spend the rest of the day and most of the night bent over, scrubbing my baby's blood off the carpet as around me, the house shakes with laughter.

KIND-HEARTED BY AMBER M. SIMPSON

Trudging down the darkening alley, Cenessa saw a small dark bird near a dumpster—seemingly injured—flapping its wings wildly as it flopped on the ground.

"Poor thing," she murmured, hurrying over. Bending down to get a better look, she found it wasn't a bird at all, but a furry black bat.

With a gasp, Cenessa stumbled back... and watched in horror as the bat rose from the ground, transforming before her eyes.

"What a kind heart you have," the tall man said, fangs sliding down from between his lips. "I bet it's delicious."

Cenessa screamed as the vampire fed.

SOUNDLESS OBLIVION BY LYDIA PRIME

No more whining, or complaining. No triple espressos with foam or fights over the color of dresses. Organic life deteriorated from the inside out. It began with the bees, but they couldn't be bothered—just as we'd suspected. Expanding our efforts to human souls, we watched as they rotted in place.

It was an absolute delight for us; bearing witness from the heavens as the third planet stopped making its ruckus. Initial angry confusion succumbed to their inevitable societal collapse. Although I believe the smarter portions of their populace had to have realized—it was a soundless oblivion they never prepared for.

A SENSELESS CRIME BY J. EDWIN BUJA

Reggie Cargille ran down the alleyway clutching the loot. Maybe this time he could avoid the peelers and gaol. The trash bins and gutters he passed stank to high heaven making Reggie gag. He daren't throw up; he couldn't afford the delay.

He paused in a doorway to catch his breath, inhaling deeply Reggie noticed that the stench was not as bad as before. In fact, it was completely gone. Realizing that there was still plenty of offal around, he sniffed. Nothing. Not a scent. He tried again. Maybe his nose was stuffed. When he stuck a finger in a nostril to check, it only went in half an inch and stopped.

He waited, listening for pursuing footsteps.

None.

Wait a second. There was no sound at all. Even the carriages and handsome cabs passing on the main street were silent. He stuck a finger in his ear to clear it. The finger didn't go in at all. Crikey! Both ears were smooth. No holes.

What the Devil?

A cat jumped out from behind a barrel, startling Reggie. He bit off the tip of his tongue then spat it out. The blood flowed freely, but where was the coppery taste?

Panicking, he ran blindly down the alley. Damnation! He was actually blind.

Reggie ran full tilt into something hard that knocked him to the ground. He felt nothing.

* * *

The crone added the Reggie doll to her growing collection. Did no one understand it was senseless to steal from a witch?

CLOSE TO SHORE BY MCKENZIE RICHARDSON

Hot sun crisps skin, coaxing sweat from pores. The call of the ocean is undeniable.

Rushing into the water, he lets the waves carry him.

Not until he feels the pull does he realize something's wrong.

Padding wildly, he tries to escape the riptide's grasp. It yanks him down, providing a glimpse of his watery captor.

The creature's mouth is massive, embedded in the sand like the seafloor itself cracking open.

Gasping, his lungs fill as the giant maw gulps

him down. Churning waters calm in his absence.

So much of the sea is unexplored, sometimes even close to shore.

DADDY'S LITTLE GIRL BY LARRY HINKLE

"Daddy!"

She cries out for me every night.

"Hurry, the bad man is coming!"

It started a few weeks ago. I've tried talking to her. Turning the lights on. Opening the closet door. Looking underneath the bed. I've asked her to sleep in my room, but she refuses to leave hers. So I made a bed on the floor and slept there. But nothing I do or say helps.

"Daddy, please!"

It's 2:00 a.m. She's been crying for nearly three hours now. I pull the covers over my head and pray she'll finally stop for the night.

I live alone.

NEVER THE SAME HAUNT BY JOHN KUJAWSKI

I was told I'd never be the same again if I saw the ghost. I was warned not to walk that one path of the woods that would lead me to her. I didn't listen, though. After all, I was a teenage boy and I thought I'd live forever.

It took a long time for me to find that legendary trail. I knew it was about a mile from a bike route and near a small pond. I had never even been to a haunted area before but I rode my bike there anyway and ventured out where the water and the trees were to see if I could see anything thrilling. For some, the woods at night might have been exciting but I wanted something more.

When I saw her appear, it was like she'd shot

out of the water. She floated by the trees and came close to me so I could get a view of her. Perhaps, just seeing the ghost could have been a life-changing experience. She had long red hair and a black dress. She was pale like a true vision of death.

At one point I could have been killed. She showed me her power and ability to move things. She sent rocks and branches flying through the air as she raised her arms. She was truly a beautiful poltergeist.

Instantly, I knew I'd never be the same. I was in love for the first time.

NO PLACE TO HIDE BY DAWN DEBRAAL

Barney knew when Angela cursed him, he was doomed. The man was daft to marry a witch. He now wondered if it were a cursed spell she put on him? One that finally wore off when he saw her for who she really was.

Deep in the woods, Angela was deep into his mind. He tried to say the ditty he recited to keep her from searching inside and finding him. but he was growing weary. He was a fool to think he could leave her. A crow cawed then another across the forest, his heart sunk.

Angela found him.

KUMIHO BY MARC SORONDO

There was a single weakness he could exploit: the ancient vixen believed him enthralled by the gleam of passion in her jade eyes and the high curve of her cheekbones. Though enthralled, he was not blind to the vulpine nature of her charms, nor could she fully conceal her tails beneath her sumptuous robes.

He waited, playing the game until she leaned in for a kiss. He knew she expected it would be his last.

Instead, he snatched the kiss, stealing her power. Swallowing it, he saw the world through fox eyes.

Enraged, the vixen swore she'd have her revenge.

THEATER GHOST BY SHANNON GRANT

The beauty and brilliance of the newly opened old theater made Marie sigh. She felt so small behind the giant blood-red curtains.

Back there was where she first saw the ghost.

She never felt threatened by her. The ghost would mind her own business, her long hair and dress floating as she scurried by in the rafters. Marie would watch her with a calm wonder.

The first time the ghost made herself known to the general public was during the opening of a children's play. Dozens of noisy, snot-nosed children grouped together in the audience, a mass of grime sitting in the classy old wood and metal seats. The field trip groups were so rowdy the actors on stage were distracted, missing lines of dialogue. One sketchy child began throwing popcorn from the front row. It was chaos, and Marie, who had been backstage watching, was getting a headache.

The ghost appeared and walked right past Marie. She gasped. This was the closest she had ever been to the specter. The noise got louder when the ghost floated out on stage in the middle of the action. The actors stopped, standing still as the ghost took over the show.

The ghost turned towards the audience and yelled a banshee's scream, her face turning from human to a horrible sunken skull, her fingers turning to bone. She rose up over the children. Then she disappeared.

The children were too scared to move for the rest of the play.

MY FOLLOWING

BY JOSHUA E. BORGMANN

I can never be alone.

I always have my secret followers.

Currently, they number twenty-seven. I know them all intimately, having spent the best times of my life with them. I assume they see things differently. I'd expected to take locks of hair as grim reminders, but I found no need. Their lifeless eyes are always watching me, and I hear them constantly. Two never stop screaming, another continues to beg while another prays for my soul.

My first smiles and says, "You deserve all of this."

I wish I'd never killed them, but tonight, another will join my following.

MEMENTO MORI BY MARY RAJOTTE

Please sit her up straight. Next to a window with the curtains drawn back. Natural light will capture the scene best.

She should wear her finest dress. Perhaps one made from dark fabric decorated at the neck with lace from an old handkerchief.

Tilt her chin down ever so slightly and apply her makeup with a light touch. A simple hairstyle. A dusting of rouge on her cheeks. A swipe of kohl on her eyelids. She should look as natural as possible to blunt the sharpness of grief.

It may take up to fifteen minutes to develop an exposure. Although it is unfathomable, the children must remain quite still. They will look notably sharper in comparison. That is normal, we assure you.

When the photograph is ready, one must be careful, as it is as delicate as life itself. Trust that this keepsake will capture her essence, and serve as a comfort during this difficult time.

Notice in the image how her eyes remain fixed and open. Please, pay them no mind. We understand it is a striking sight, but one that is not uncommon. Often, we paint them on the photo negative before the image is processed to give the subject the illusion of life. Other times, it is simply a natural occurrence, one we did not notice until afterward, it seems.

Please accept our most sincere condolences. She seems a lively spirit, incontent to remain in memory alone, one who shall linger long after this cherished memento withers.

MIRROR IMAGE BY NICOLE HENNING

Staggering across the room she scratched at her arms anxiously. Every reflective surface had been covered with dark sheets or scratched with sandpaper. She had stopped going into the rest of the apartment a few days ago, she couldn't tell how many.

The floor under her bare feet creaked while she walked back and forth. She couldn't remember the last time she had eaten. She had stopped because when she went into the kitchen she could hear scratchy laughter behind the dark blankets covering the chrome refrigerator.

Feeling a wave of dizziness she tripped and fell into the wall and drug the blanket off of the mirror that was attached to the door. When she sat up she screamed as a distorted version of her reflection reached out from the mirrors rippling surface and pulled her into it.

WITCH'S BREW BY CHISTO HEALY

Jonathon watched Mary dropping something into the pot steaming on the stovetop. He smiled and stepped forward, looking over her shoulder.

"What are you making, honey?"

Mary didn't so much as glance back at him. She seemed lost in thought. Jonathon noticed her mouth was moving. His brow furrowed. He looked down into the pot and saw a feather, bones, rocks of some kind, and what looked like swirls of blood. He cringed.

"Jesus, what are you doing, making some kind of magic spell?" He laughed nervously.

"Precisely," Mary said, finally turning to face him.

Jonathon's eyes went wide and he seized his chest, fingers like claws. His open mouth released a hoarse croak and then he dropped to the floor where he twitched for a moment before laying still.

Mary removed the pot from the stove and turned the burner off. Her foot hit the pedal to open the trash can and she emptied the contents of the pot into the can before letting the lid fall closed. She placed the empty pot back on the stovetop. Then she looked calmly down at Jonathon's face, frozen in agony.

"Never cheat on a witch," she said.

HAUNTED BY RJ MELDRUM

The house was reportedly haunted. People had gone missing after visiting it. Dave insisted that he and Julie check it out. They explored, finding nothing spookier than spider webs. They stood in the bedroom.

"This was where the murder took place. This is where the ghost walks."

Julie was unimpressed.

"I want to go home."

It was near sunset; it was getting hard to see.

"Let's go."

They headed downstairs. In the darkness of the hallway, Dave reached out for the door. It took a moment for him to realize there was no longer a handle, no longer a door.

EYES OPENED WIDE BY RADAR DEBOARD

Dominic dropped the ancient tome on his work desk as the swirling winds picked up in the tiny office.

He gasped in utter shock as a hole began to open wide in the middle of the floor.

His curiosity pushed him towards the edge of the newly opened vortex. Peering down into the endless pit, Dominic was met by the sight of unimaginable horrors bathed in the glow of hellfire. Demons began to climb up the sides of the pit, making their way towards Dominic.

"It's all real," he gasped as he fell to his knees,

"Hell really does exist."

RECLAIM BY CHRIS BANNOR

The Goddess filled her sight, and she lifted her hands and head to the Ever-Blessed Realm. There was no higher calling than to receive the Goddess and she was overcome with pride at having been chosen, of all the possible girls, to hold the Goddess for even a moment.

The awe fell away to a stifling, choking sensation though, and fear began to replace her joy as she slipped from existence. The Goddess had a taste of the human world now, and it was time for her return.

Time to take back her tainted lands.

Time to reclaim her throne.

GH19 BY
DAVID SIMMS

"Everyone, keep your masks and glasses on! These are sneaky bastards." The ghost tour guide grinned and carried his lantern through the asylum halls.

Lewis snorted, thinking of his rights. "Whoa!" A whisp of white streamed across the hallway in the abandoned asylum, so he pulled the Nikon to his plastic lenses, bouncing off without the focus he required.

"Fuck this," he said, pushing the glasses off. Nobody noticed.

The flash drew the infection straight into his nostrils. It streamed like a backward sneeze straight up into his skull.

He shook it off, denying such a contagion could be real. Those who believed would be the first ones to wear masks in schools, keep the six-feet rule, and wash their hands after peeing.

A slight chill coursed through him and Lewis coughed for the first time. The scream barreled up through his lungs in a viscous howl, rolling from his mouth onto the carpet between his feet with the tones of a geriatric choir.

The next ghost wrenched his jaws open with a fetid stench. Voices echoed between his ears.

"Thank you," they said in a discordant chorus, a series of deadened tones.

Lewis struggled through the halls as each cell germinated into what it once had been ages ago Souls long constrained, breathed. Lives burgeoned forth, blossoming into fresh voices.

When the group exited the tour, Lewis watched his body step through the doorway. The virus had left him behind. It had so much to share with the world.

IN HOUND SIT BY M. BETTERELLI

"Big" Phil Iverson drove his eighteen-wheeler down Interstate Ten a little past midnight. The monotonous white line fever struck him, as tiredness plagued his eyes. The audible sound of the rumble strip jolted him back to the road noticing he'd nodded off. Both eyes darted back and forth attempting to stay alert. Out of nowhere, a large black dog jumped in front of the truck. Phil swerved violently hoping to miss it. Stopping the truck he preceded to exit and check for possible damage, along with blood or fur on the grill. Surprised, there was nothing.

Phil pulled himself back into the truck and situated himself ready to drive once again. He rubbed his eyes thinking to himself.

I'll just take it to the next rest stop. At that moment a low growling came from the sleeper and gleaming orange eyes appeared. Phil slowly turned his head only to see the shadowy beast of a dog's snarling lips and exposed teeth come lunging at him.

Blood sprayed the windshield and interior of the truck as Phil fought something that appeared larger than a wolf, but had no tangible form. He opened the door attempting to escape but his blood loss was too great as he felt the fatigue of death approach. His eyes rolled towards the back of his head as he fell sideways out of the truck. The shadowy beast followed him out, snatched him up, and dragged him off into the night.

INTO THE WOODS BY SOPHIE WAGNER

Mia's eyes snapped open as she was shaken awake in the middle of the night. She blinked laboriously, trying to rid the sleep grit from her eyes.

"Hurry up!" Her mother shrieked. "We have to go! We're not safe here anymore."

Mia opened her mouth to protest but stopped when she saw the urgency and fear etched into her mother's face.

Quickly, she jumped out of bed and followed her out of the bedroom and down the stairs. The darkness of the hallway uneased her greatly and a horrible chemical smell assaulted her nostrils as she ran. Sulfur maybe?

Yet there was no time to stop and think about it for they were already at the front door.

Without hesitation, her mother threw the door open with such force that it looked as though it might break off of its hinges. They ran into the night, heading straight for the woods behind the house.

Mia tried to keep up even though she could barely even see her mother anymore. But her lungs felt like they were on fire and her feet were bleeding from the sticks underfoot.

Suddenly, a terrible ripping noise sounded behind her. Mia quickly turned around to see her mother. Yet, it was no longer her mother. A bloody and horned demon ripped the skin suit of her mother off of itself.

"She made a good host, but not as good as you will."

STRANDED BY P.J. BLAKEY-NOVIS

It was meant to be an enjoyable excursion to celebrate our first wedding anniversary. The light aircraft came down during a storm, killing the pilot and my wife on impact, seven weeks ago. I never even considered eating them until it was too late, having buried them beside the wreckage. God only knew where I'd ended up, or if help would come.

When I first heard the singing, I swore it was my imagination but followed the sound regardless. When I saw her face, I couldn't move.

"You're dead," I mumbled, fearing insanity. She didn't reply, simply pulling the torn clothing from her body. Taking me in her embrace, she undressed me. She felt cold and she tasted different, saltier perhaps. Her body brought with it an unpleasant smell, but I hadn't washed for weeks so didn't dare to say anything.

Despite my concerns, we made frantic love on the beach, taking each other in every way possible. When our desires had been satisfied, I lay my head on her chest, nestled between her breasts, hearing no heartbeat, feeling no breaths being taken.

"You're dead," I repeated, looking into her now misty-grey eyes.

"I never said I wasn't," she replied.

KITCHEN WITCH BY PATRICK WINTERS

Her grandmother had given her the doll as a child.

"This is a good witch," she'd said. "It'll protect you from a very bad one. Keep it always." And she'd done just that, more out of fondness than superstition, the doll watching over her from its shelf in her kitchen.

But when she came home one day, the doll had fallen to the floor; her Pomeranian had torn it to shreds.

She set to cleaning up the mess, feeling saddened by the ruined memento. But sadness became fear when she heard a cold, creaking voice from over her shoulder:

"*Finally....*"

LAST TESTAMENT BY DONNA MARIE WEST

After weeks of searching for her dying grandfather's last will and testament, Rachel had taken the evening to distribute Halloween treats.

"I'm all out," she called, answering the doorbell at eight-fifteen.

But there were no costumed children standing on the porch, bags open to collect their candies. Instead, she found a skeletal old man wearing a charcoal suit and red bow tie.

"Gramps! What—"

Without a word, the figure withdrew a thick

envelope from his pocket and handed it to her

She ripped it open to extract the missing testament. Her voice shaking with confusion, she said, "Come inside," then turned away to pull her buzzing cell from her pocket.

"I'm so sorry, Rachel," her dad said in a thick voice, "but your Gramps passed away tonight."

Rachel stared at the now vacant front porch, her blood running cold. "I know."

TEN POINTS
BY SCOTT
MCGREGOR

Inside my tent, I tried my hardest to read but the wind made it difficult to focus. Whenever I couldn't sleep, I'd simply read a book until I drifted off to sleep. So, even on my camping trip with Tia, I brought a book in case of such an emergency. Every minute, the lamplight diminished slightly.

Let's go camping, Tia said. *It'll be fun,* she said. Between my sore feet, the hours we spent pitching a tent, and the awful s'mores, Tia's idea of fun was crap. Still, the story regarding the camping grounds mildly interested me. As the legend goes, an ancient spirit haunts them, punishing those who enter. Of course, I didn't believe it, as it sounded like something coined by a thirteen-year-old who recently watched *The Blair Witch*

Project.

The wind intensified, and the roof of my tent brushed against my head. Once it reached my shoulders, I lay on my back. The tent continued to bow inwards, and two-thirds of the way down, I got a tad nervous. I glanced away from my book, watching the wind pushing onto my tent. Maybe my eyes deceived me, but I counted ten points pressing onto the tent, almost like fingers.

Eventually, the lamplight faded, and for the rest of the night, I stayed awake, waiting to see if the tent would collapse.

The next morning, I left my tent and found two hand prints plastered onto the outside.

HUNGER
BY DAWN
DEBRAAL

Gloria could see her breath. Dampness ran in rivulets down the walls. She was chained to the ceiling of the cave. The last thing she remembered was meeting Benjamin in the Good Times Saloon. He bought her a drink, was it drugged? A creaking door opened.

"Ahh, you have awakened my love." Benjamin closed the door behind him. There was something different about him. Something she hadn't noticed before.

"Please, let me go," Gloria begged.

Benjamin looked at her with hunger in his eyes, throwing back his head in laughter, he exposed his fangs when coming in for the kill.

FUCKIN' GHOSTS BY KEVIN J. KENNEDY

Ghosts freak me out. Why the fuck would you stay behind on this planet if there was somewhere else to go. Unfinished shit… bullshit!

I don't give a fuck if I'm murdered. I'm straight onto the next plane of existence to see what the fuck is going on. You can take this life and stick it right up your arse. I've been going to seances for a while. There was even the odd one that I almost believed but never a sign of a ghost. I started staying in the 'most haunted' hotels and castles.

Another sham. Never seen a single specter.

I was beginning to think it was a lost cause,

then I found a little witch's shop in Scotland. The Green Witch it was called. It was in a tiny village called Aberdour. I went inside and the witch was sitting in an old-fashioned chair, covered in shawls. She was next to a roaring fire. She waved me into the chair opposite and threw some powder in the fire. It roared and then pictures began to dance.

I saw friends and family I had lost. There were old work colleagues that had passed on, and acquaintances that were no longer with us. They whispered to me. 'Do it, kill yourself, you're better off with us.'

I've taken the pills now; I've drunk the Whisky.

I hope I go fast.

I really fucking hope I don't end up stuck here as a ghost.

THE HAG OF HILDALAND BY JOSHUA E. BORGMANN

Among the Finfolk, I was once known as the greatest beauty of Hildaland. I could have had my pick of any of the fishermen along the Orkney shores. They would have paid good silver for me to carry them away.

I should have taken even the lowest of them, but I thought myself a rebel and took a Finfolk husband. After seven years, my beauty began to fade faster than from the human wives. Seven years later, I no longer recognized myself. My husband claimed a new human wife and that miserable slave laughed as she called me the hag.

HIGH SURF ADVISORY

B.F. VEGA

During the winter, we get advisories of danger-ous surf. Sometimes they close the beaches by blocking off the highway. That never bothered us. We walked to the ocean every day anyway.

That night, we could hear the waves getting closer to us. Finally, we could just make out the white water splashing at the foot of the bluff we were on.

"What's that?" Alicia asked, pointing down to where the beach used to be.

There was a woman walking along. We could see her clearly. Her dress was white, her hair was black and she walked just above the water that was four-inch deep at that point.

We were on our feet immediately.

"We should go investigate," Alicia said

"We can't even get there." I pointed out.

"Come on, we've lived here all our lives, we know what to watch out for. Let's just get a little closer."

Alicia started down the long steep path to the beach. The woman seemed to see us then and started walking toward the path. She got to Alicia and disappeared.

Alicia turned to us as if to say "Did you see that?"

I tried to warn her. Alicia couldn't hear me as the sleeper wave came in.

They never found her body but, I heard a story recently that on nights when the beaches are closed, two women walk where there is no sand.

HIGHLAND HUNTER BY NATASHA SINCLAIR

The huntsman tracked in circles; thrill for blood intensifying. She could feel it, beady eyes observing from above. Just a curious corvid to be paid no mind.

Hoofprints like breadcrumbs, she scattered strategically around his camp. By nightfall, his desire for blood would lend to feed hers. Unsated, frustration befell his air.

Owls hooted, nocturnal beasts scuttled; swooping from her perch, the Baobhan Siths' black feathers transformed. The cloven cloaked beauty pulsing with unfettered blood-lust went to her hunter; a paradigm shift.

Mysterious stranger, the highland reaper. The faux prey mounted the hunter, she'd hunted—mercilessly draining him dry—screaming.

THE PHANTOM MOO BY SHANNON GRANT

"Mooooooo."

The bellow echoed throughout the abandoned locale, waking Kip. He left the fog of sleep behind and stretched. Sunlight streamed through the window, lighting the office where he had slept.

Leo had made his bed on one of the conveyor belts. Kip thought about it for a few hot seconds but decided it was too much. They were both into weird exploration shit, but Leo was the crazier of the two, and Kip suspected sleeping on the conveyer belt of an abandoned slaughterhouse was one of Leo's actual bucket list items.

"Moooooo."

Like a See and Say toy. The arrow spins. The cow goes *moooooo.*

Kip rose, still wearing his boots. He wasn't about to take them off in a place like this. He thought about the lockers and wondered which one had belonged to "Burger" Bob Creedy, the worker who had died there shortly before the place had closed.

"Mooooooo."

People said the place was haunted.

Kip walked down the stairs leading to the floor where the machinery was. Leo still lay upon the conveyer belt. Now there was a man standing over him.

"Mooooooo," the man said and Kip recognized him as Bob Creedy. His face was raw hamburger.

Kip's stomach turned when the man looked up and grinned at him. The man was dead, Kip had seen the pictures of him after he had been dragged through the machinery.

Bob grinned as he reached out and flipped a nearby switch.

The conveyer belt began to move.

WITCH BALL BY RUTHANN JAGGE

Claire poked at the ornament hanging in her bedroom window, a birthday gift from Aunt Mary, who claimed it was magic. Suspended by the length of clear fishing-line her Dad used to secure it, the colors swirled with every movement.

"It's a Witch Ball. To protect you." Aunt Mary proclaimed as Claire pushed it away, eager for another gift. She nodded her thanks, secretly thinking it was strange.

Not long after her celebration, he followed Claire home for the first time. He liked the way her ponytail bounced as she walked. He drove slowly, snapping photo after photo, he would be patient.

Claire waved to her parents as they drove away, she looked forward to being alone for the weekend. She curled up on her bed with some favorite snacks and a book, intending to read, but dozed off instead.

The rusted metal screeched when he opened her bedroom window. Claire sat up, startled to see a large man pushing his way through the opening. She screamed but as his feet hit the floor, the bauble swinging above circled his head rapidly. He looked at her and started to speak, but the glass sphere sliced neatly through his neck.

In an instant, he was gone. The colorful strands danced furiously as they absorbed his body and dark soul, adding them to the other demons trapped within the sparkling glass ball.

SYMPATHY FOR THE OLD OAK BY NIC BRADY

Desolate and alone stood what was once an old oak tree. Spread out was its extremities that had been sawn off. It is Autumn and leaves, branches, and other foliage has impregnated the tree, wrapping around, strangling what was left of the oak.

Growing moss was weaving in and out, she screams a silent scream of agony. With each breath she takes her body becomes red and bloody. It wants revenge on the chainsaw that all but killed her.

A roar of a giant blade catches her attention, the suffering takes over and the wielder begins a wild dance with the Oak.

She gently weeps.

The heart is palpable. It pulsates as the chainsaw works to cut off the overgrown branches... The limbs of the tree.

As the chainsaw wielder climbs down the ladder he had propped up against the oak, she comes alive and grabs him by the leg, severing an appendage for each time he took one of hers. The tree ran out of branches, but it was thirsty.

With a deep burp, she is vengeful, death becomes her and the starvation continues...

Now, known as the old widow, fear runs through the townsfolk. But the tree is now a beast and coming for them.

ONE NIGHT STAND BY RJ MELDRUM

By the time they got to her apartment, his passion had waned. The nightclub had been dark, he hadn't realized she was so thin. Her skin was sallow, her eyes sunken. The bones protruded through the flesh on her face. He decided to leave.

"Sorry, I have to be somewhere."

"It's because I'm thin, isn't it? I need you to stay."

"I have to go."

She blocked him.

"I need to feed."

She rammed her index fingers into his eye sockets. After a few moments, she started to eat.

Her flesh filled out and the color returned to her cheeks.

A GOOD GRANDMOTHER BY RADAR DEBOARD

Samuel sat with the blanket pulled up to his shoulders as he waited for his grandmother to come in.

His grandma had tucked him into bed since he was able to walk. She was a good grandmother. Always reading bedtime stories, or bringing him a warm glass of milk to help him sleep better. Samuel could count on his grandma every night.

There was just one glaring problem.

His grandma had died six days ago.

Yet, as Samuel looked to his open bedroom door he saw her standing there.

"Grandma?" he squeaked as the decaying figure stepped into the room.

THE BAD CHILD BY TERRY MILLER

The bad child is always in his room. Always. That's the way the story goes. To this day, the room remains bolted shut from the outside. Visitors say, at night, you can still hear the sobbing and sniffling behind the door; sixty years of tears, fallen to the wooden floor.

The last tour of the evening, a bit of curiosity struck Bobby Evans. He could barely reach the latch but he managed. The door lightly creaked. No one was inside. What a rip-off!

That night, Mrs. Evans passed by Bobby's closed bedroom door, the sobs and sniffles broke her heart.

VLAD THE IMPALER BY GABRIELLA BALCOM

Clattering hoofbeats echoed as Vlad rode through Wallachia, his army following. He smiled, anticipating tonight's victory banquet.

The feuding boyars arrived by the hundreds, feasting eagerly.

Vlad had them impaled alive. Dipping bread in their blood, he ate with gusto, savoring their flesh, too.

Later, he luxuriated in a tub of blood.

Droplets rose, floating in midair and transforming into glowing fairies. Baring their jagged teeth, they latched onto his body. They ignored his bellows, sucking his blood and biting off chunks of flesh.

Vlad's servants came running but discovered only skeletal remains covered in bite marks in the tub.

DARK DESCENT BY MARINA SCHNIERER

Lights flicker, dark shadows dart across the room, an icy cold sensation moves through me. I walk the lonely halls of this old mansion tense, feeling its blood-curdling chill.

I sense its need to break me, this presence that lingers, waiting, taunting, suffocating. Day after day, night after night, a never-ending cycle.

Fear entwined with loneliness and regret, yet I cannot break away. It started as a dare, but an obsession it has become.

All-consuming, torturing my thoughts and emotions, a maddening descent into insanity.

Doomed for all eternity as I become a part of its darkness, like a piece of an ever-growing puzzle, and I will await its next victim as the others did before me.

THE MAGIC KNOWS (THE BLOODY PRICE) BY CHRIS BANNOR

I stare at the front of the room as the circle opens before me. They are holding me back before I can try to breakthrough.

Power floods my senses the moment the spell accepts the sacrifice, as my daughter's blood drips from bound wrists. Words I don't know spill from my lips in time with my daughter, holding onto life by the thread of this spell. The coven made my sacrifice and tried to pass it off as a gift.

The magic knows, though. The coven isn't

given strength; I am.

And they will bathe in blood for it.

THROUGH THE AIR BY MIRIAM H. HARRISON

The snail slid along, not quite on the ground. As she watched it move through the air, she wasn't sure where it had come from, how it had gotten in. Maybe, like her, it was looking for shelter, a safe place away from the predatory things outside. Those things that had never been given wings yet now filled the skies with teeth and claws, emboldened by flight.

She could hear people's screams. Fists pounded on the door, but too late—already she could hear the sounds of bloody death. She covered her ears and cowered on the floor, looking only at the snail and its soothing path through the air.

SILENCE IS GOLDEN BY NICOLE HENNING

Their parents couldn't understand what had happened. One morning they woke up to discover one of their twin girls, Jamie, could no longer speak while her sister, Jane, was fine. They took her to every specialist they could find and the conclusion was always the same. It was psychosomatic, her vocal cords were healthy and there was no physical cause for her muteness. One night, they left the girls home alone, they were teenagers after all and able to care for themselves, regardless of Jamie's affliction.

After they left, Jane smiled and began to torment Jamie, calling her names and pushed her into their bedroom closet. The night Jamie had lost her voice Jane had shoved her into the closet and made her sleep there. When she got out in the morning her voice was gone. After five minutes, Jane heard high laughter coming from the closet, and thinking Jamie's voice had returned ran to the door.

When their parents returned they found Jane rocking back and forth on the bedroom floor unable to see. Jamie however talked excitedly about the old woman that you could see through who lived in the closet and how she had borrowed her voice and now she had Janes's eyes.

NEON RAIN BY TODD LOVE

Cole never felt the cold of the sidewalk or the chill of the rain pooling in the concaves of his lifeless eyes. The red neon sign flickered to life hiding the red that flowed freely from the back of Cole's now open skull. If Cole's eyes had been open, he would have witnessed a familiar face smiling as it vanished over the edge of the roof.

An invisible light broke through the darkness and all that was Cole emerged from the shell that held his soul captive.

"You pushed me," Cole whispered.

"So we could be together," the murderer replied.

"We broke up years ago!" Cole yelled.

A hand reached out untouched by the rain. Eyes that could not meet his looked down at the red neon reflection in the shallow pool of rainwater they were standing in.

"I did it for us. You promised we would be together no matter what." Cole heard the truth in her voice and felt the shame hit his heart.

The front door to the apartment building flew open allowing the scream that was being restrained by the glass to escape. The neon sign shook and fell to the sidewalk in an explosion causing the rain to transform into a brilliant white flash of light. Cole was gone. A woman reached for Cole and placed his rain-soaked head on her lap.

A scream no one living heard echoed in a realm that was haunted by those who could not move on.

CONSUMPTION
BY DAVID SIMMS

She slid off me after the convulsions ceased. An electric shock, akin to static cling, tugged at my flesh. Smiling, the being rose up in a bluish haze, the sensations just tangible moments before already fading into a hazy memory.

Not much of me remained.

Tomorrow... she whispered, dissipating before me.

Later, I gathered the energy to roll off the bed to clean myself up. My legs barely supported me, failing the first time. Once muscular calves had withered, bulging thighs flaccid, yet moved me to the bathroom.

Staring into the mirror, the tears streamed once more from rheumy eyes. I ran a shaky hand through the remaining shock of white hair. Just two weeks ago, I had moved into this house straight out of college.

It took only one night for her to find me. My roommates never heard the screams – because there had been none.

The ravishing creature attacked me that first night, shredding my clothes and holding my arms down with spectral limbs. She was beautiful, translucent hair flowing around an angelic face that bored into me with eyes that emoted a hunger I'd never experienced. Her body wrapped itself around mine and engulfed me, sucking me into her, riding me for what felt like days. Afterward, I woke to find her gone, with only the remains of her phantom-like fuck covering me.

Now she had returned. In throes of ecstasy, she tore my soul from me, into whatever she was.

And I ceased to be, with a smile.

TURNING BY MEERA DANDEKAR

"Who is there?" He bit on his lip. "What do you want?"

The cupboard hid someone inside. The clock reflected three minutes away from striking three, never moving.

The boy moved closer, a bat in his hand, ready to swing. The windows were open, it was a windy night.

"Come out," He cried.

The cupboard opened.

It was empty.

The boy moved back, then forward. His hands reached for the doors in an attempt to close them. The doors pushed him inside the dark space.

He didn't realize he was floating.

A girl entered her room, sucking on her thumb. He beat on the closed doors.

She held her hands to her ears. He didn't realize he was haunting *her*.

THE CURIOUS CASE OF SHADOW MAN BY DAVID O. HUGHES

They say he roams the streets, alleys, and roads at night, and that he can be seen skulking around graveyards, homes, and the like– peeping in windows for people to snatch.

Children are his favorite, but an elitist he is not.

He gobbles up his prey in shadow puppets, cast off floors and walls like traps, before dropping them in his bag and taking them to his depths. Never to be seen again.

Their bones have built his palaces; their eyes have studded his crowns.

Is he a ghost, or is he man?

Nobody knows for he dwells in darkness....

WE LIVE HERE NOW

BY SHANNON GRANT

Eli stood there stunned, his mind trying to process what had gone down the night before.

Milo stood beside him, looking down at their collapsed tent.

"Well," Milo said, "It looks like we live here now."

Eli's head snapped up to look directly at Milo. "What the hell do you mean by that?"

"Exactly what I said," he countered. "Whatever happened last night means we live here now."

Eli searched his memory for the previous night's events. He stared at the tent, ripped apart, hoping it would dislodge the boulders in the way of his memory. There was a bear. There might've been a bear? He remembered hot breath and claws tearing. A growl. A scream. Milo's scream.

After that, darkness. Then, painful sunlight waking him.

"My body is under there," Milo said, pointing to the tent. "Yours is in the weeds over there." He gestured towards the woods.

"You can't be serious." Eli was done. He stomped over to the weeds and looked down. The rocks inside his head finally moved so the memory of the night could flood back. He had tried to crawl away after the bear had clawed his back. Eli's bloodied and mutilated body stretched out on the ground under him. the

"So, yeah," Milo yelled. "Get the picture yet? We're ghosts, dumbass. We LIVE here now."

DUST TO DUST

BY DAWN DEBRAAL

Anthony's mind raced. Human remains this far from the original settlement Were these the bodies of nomads from the tribe or members who had been banished? They had been carefully preserved. The sarcophagus was gently lifted from the tomb.

"We will wait until we are in London to open it," he told his fellow excavators.

While everyone was asleep. Anthony found himself called to open the sarcophagus knowing he shouldn't but longing to know the content.

As he pried at the cover, a cloud enveloped Anthony reducing him to dust, pulling him into the coffin to lie beside the queen.

FALLEN BY WONDRA VANIAN

An explosion of sound rang through the church. Startled awake, Father McKinley fell out of bed and ran to the nave in his stocking feet. He slid to a stop just short of the rubble that had once been the building's roof. An enormous black feather floated down on an eddy of dust.

The pile of concrete shifted. A trembling hand reached up, found purchase, and heaved itself through the debris. The naked man glowed slightly in the dim room.

Could it be…? It *had* to be…

Father McKinley thrilled at the possibility. He clutched his suddenly tight chest. Believing and *seeing* were two different things.

An angel! Praise the…

The glowing man turned to look around, revealing ragged, bloody tears across his back. The light emanating from his skin slowly faded. Only the fire in his furious scarlet gaze remained.

"Oh, God," Father McKinley whispered without thinking. The... no, he couldn't call the creature what his heart knew it to be. It turned to face him. Lowering its head, it smiled menacingly in a way that promised retribution for every sermon made, every prayer raised.

Father McKinley knew he should have run. He also knew that, even if he had, he wouldn't have stood a chance. As it was, all he could do was stare at the horns protruding from the creature's head. The old priest had time for just one thought before it descended upon him and his heart gave out.

Even the Devil was once an angel...

WRONG WAY
BY RJ MELDRUM

Kate never usually walked through the underpass, but she was in a rush. As she descended towards the tunnel she sensed someone behind her. It was a man.

"Stop!" he called.

She sped up.

At the other end of the underpass, she saw a female figure. Kate ran towards her. As she got closer, she realized something wasn't right. The skin on her face was loose, sagging. Kate stopped. The creature, realizing it'd been discovered, reached up and removed its mask. Kate saw red eyes and teeth. She started to run, back towards the man.

Unfortunately, the creature was faster.

THE SLEEPWALKER BY ARCHIT JOSHI

I stared proudly at my pedometer app, at the badge that celebrated me having reached my doctor's recommended daily steps. Fifteen thousand.

"You need something physically taxing to wear you down," he'd said. "I can only give you so many pills. Be exhausted when you hit the bed. You'll be out like a light all night."

That had been a week ago. Today was the first time I'd reached 15K. My weary eyes watched as a changing calendar reset my steps of the day to zero.

* * *

I woke up restless. The doctor's advice was bull. I'd gone to bed exhausted *and* woke up the same way. My ears, distantly aware of low murmurs. Come to think of it, I'd been hearing murmurs all through the night. But this was real, right outside my window.

A crowd had gathered below my neighbor's house. I dressed, rinsed my mouth of morning breath, and joined them.

"Lola was killed last night," a stranger whispered to me in response to my enquiring expression.

"Horrifically too," someone added. "Throat slit, ears lopped off and stuffed in the mouth."

How can this not *be my morning tweet?*

I rushed back to the iPhone tucked under my pillow. It unlocked the pedometer widget on my home screen.

The widget showed two-hundred and forty-three steps. There was blood at the corners of my screen.

ROSIE BY MELODY E. MCINTYRE

"The baby's already asleep. Thanks again for watching him last minute. I really need this shift," said Ann as she rushed out.

I sat on the couch, ready for an easy night with Netflix and a baby monitor. A small girl padded her way into the room.

"I'm cold," she said and coughed.

"What's your name?" I asked. Ann had only mentioned the baby.

"Rosie."

"I'm Leticia. Come sit on the couch, Rosie."

Rosie climbed up and I hurried around the house collecting all the blankets I could find. Her cough worsened and no matter how many blankets I brought, she wouldn't stop shivering. Finally, I climbed onto the couch and held her tight. I gasped at the iciness of her skin. As I held her, she grew warm, but my body began to grow cold. By the time Ann came home, I was freezing and coughing and Rosie was sleeping soundly.

I met Ann in the kitchen and through chattering teeth told her how well behaved they both were and then led her back to the living room and an empty couch.

"Rosie was the daughter of the couple who lived here before me. She went missing one winter night and they moved away. Sometimes I hear coughing in the night and wake up feeling a chill. Leticia, you okay? You're turning blue."

But I couldn't answer her. All I could think about was the icy cold that wouldn't let me go.

DOLLFACE BY TERRY MILLER

Tiny steps littered the silence, slow and soft they continued in repetition. The wood floors of the hall refused to conceal the smallest of disturbances. Rachel's door crept open, the carpeted floor of her room muffled her visitor's entrance.

The cover at the foot of her bed rose, a small form slithered beneath to the head and rested its own upon the pillow adjacent to Rachel's. Her eyes opened, the streetlight outside her window illuminated the pale, dirty face staring back at her through empty pits; the face of the doll whose eyes she had gouged out as a child.

CLEAN CUT BY RUTHANN JAGGE

Abby always jogged the same trails to track her time. The community park was small but safe. She preferred an evening workout.

He was tall and lanky, walking loosely in her direction, wearing a black hoody pulled up to cover his face. He was considerate given the circumstances.

Abby nodded as he passed, "Have a good one."

He moved away without raising his head. *What a jerk*, rolling her eyes.

She noticed him again, a week later, sitting on a bench intended for bird-watchers. He was wearing the same oversized hoody. She could see his face: he was clean-cut and good looking!

I'm so curious, Abby thought, *it's damn hard to meet cute guys*. She walked closer, tapping at her watch to appear less obvious.

"Hey there, how was your walk?" He looked up: he was fair with dark eyes. Blonde hair that was stylish but in need of a wash.

"Hello, I'm Abby."

No reply as he pulled the black hood up over his head. She couldn't think of anything else to say, obviously he wasn't interested. Abby sighed, then noticed the thick dirt caked on his shoes. Dirty hands also, he was covered in soil, as if he had rolled in or out of it.

He lunged at her, Abby smelled moss and rot. His filthy mouth covered her scream as he sucked the life from her. Even the dead need to eat.

REFLECTIONS BY JOSHUA LUPARDUS

"Who is real?
Which is which?
Look in the mirror,
And you'll be switched."

She read the warning
But didn't care.
She looked directly
To fix her hair.

The mirror cracked,
Long lines across.

The real girl trapped.
The reflection lost.

Her shadow bent,
At an angle wrong,
Toward the light,
She don't belong.

The specter flowed
Down through the hall.
She looked for others
To them she called.

An older woman met her soon,
Behind her smile darkness loomed.
The reflection girl led her away,
And smashed her through some glass that day.

Her reflection was not freed,
Though her soul passed by swiftly.
The windows glass could not release
The other hidden entities.

She continued on her murderous spree,
Trying to find a way to free,
Other reflections who 'were trapped like me',
But always found it could not be.

Her portal was the only one
That could undo what had been done.
To free those trapped who were inside,
Was a futile effort of her time.

Her crimes were done.
The house abandoned.
But she went back,
A bit more maddened.

She slammed her fists against the glass
Cracks appeared there really fast.
The real girl cried out on the other side
But she reached out and the crack got wide.

They switched places once again,
The reflection freed from her life of sin.

The real girl soon was put in jail,

For the murders, they set no bail.

DO NOT DISTURB BY SHANNON GRANT

I wasn't sure what they were.

My flashlight hit the small objects on the ground. Some were square, all sharp angles and symmetry. Some were long and pointed towards the night sky. Others resembled people with cute elven faces and wings sprouting out from their backs.

This forest was magic. But sometimes it could be a confusing magic.

I knelt to get a better look at the objects, taking care not to place my knees on any of them. Most of them had writing and carvings on them, but I couldn't tell what they meant. I picked up one of them, a small white block, and brought it up to my eyes. The flashlight beam illuminated it.

Still couldn't tell what it was.

I placed it back where it had been.

A shriek sounded out in the night.

My heart leaped up in my throat. A strange glow began to radiate from the object I had put down, then traveling to the others.

This spot grew colder than it had been before.

Then they began to rise.

The winged creatures came out of the ground, so many spectral shapes glowing. Some began to dart around, swishes of light. Others hovered, and one came up to my face.

It was a skeleton body with wings. The skull grinned at me, then gave a giggle. It made my nerves jangle. I rose, finally releasing what this place was.

It was a fairy cemetery, and I had disturbed the dead.

WAR BY B. A. NIELSEN

The burning sensation of toxic smoke filled her lungs and she smiled. This region had once been a picture of peace and pure tranquility until the day War convinced the natives to reclaim the land she had told them was once theirs.

Now, as she walked amongst the bodies of what had become a war-torn community, her sister fell into step with her.

"Nice work, Big Red," said Death.

War couldn't suppress her pride, which was short-lived as corpses around her started to rise, gasping for air.

"What the hell are you doing?" demanded War.

"I'm fucking with you, Sis."

THE MAMALARANG BY PATRICK WINTERS

The corporal tossed and turned in his cot, wishing for home and a chesty blonde.

He was hot, sweating, and itching all over. That wasn't out of the ordinary, though– not in the Luzon.

But when all the prickling wouldn't ease up, he glared down at his legs and saw all the little beetles that were bursting out of his pores and crawling across his skin, leaving thin trails of blood in their wake.

He screamed, and the rest of the camp started to scream along with him.

From somewhere within the rainforest, the *Mamalarang* laughed, pleased with her mischief.

NIGHT DRIVE
BY RJ MELDRUM

He woke, disturbed. The dream had been vivid, violent. Their car had crashed; metal, glass, and flesh, all ripped apart. His mood changed when he saw everything was the same. The same road, the same darkness. His wife was still driving, staring out the windshield into the night.

"I just had the strangest dream."

She didn't answer.

"I dreamt we crashed. That we died."

She turned to look at him. The front of her face was a bloodied mess, her eyes missing. Blood oozed out of her wounds. She grinned with a toothless mouth.

"That was no dream, my love."

DANGED CAT BY DONNA MARIE WEST

"Might be it's rabid," Pa said after shooting the cougar that attacked me. It snarled and bounded into the woods. He never found it.

A month passed. My wounds healed with no sign of illness. I had some trouble sleeping, but put that down to shock and stress.

I got up tonight to open the window for fresh air. The sky was clear, the full moon bright.

My throat tightened. Hot pain shot through my entire body. Looking down to see tawny fur sprouting from my arms and chest, I thought,

Danged cat wasn't rabid. It was something far worse.

STARING AT THE SHADOWS BY RADAR DEBOARD

Juan had no choice but to keep his eyes focused on the large shadow at the end of the hall. The inhuman shape of it sent an uneasy chill up his spine.

Taking in a deep breath, he turned off the hall light for a few seconds. He quickly flipped it back on to see that the shadow was closer than before.

Close enough that he could make out the shape of claws, razor-sharp teeth, and inhuman appendages in the shadow. Juan noticed the light starting to flicker.

Taking in a deep breath, he waited for darkness

to envelop him.

AFTERWORD

Thank you for reading our macabre drabbles collection and we hope you enjoyed it! If you did, or even if not, if you could take a moment to write a short review it is always appreciated! You can find us on Goodreads here!

If you enjoyed this collection by the Macabre Ladies you can also check more of our work:

<u>Holiday Horror Collection</u>

Dark X-Mas

Dark Valentine

Dark Solstice

Dark Celebration

Dark Halloween

Holiday Horror Box Set

<u>**Drabbles of Dread Collection**</u>

Drabbles of Dread

Extreme Drabbles of Dread

Coming soon from the Macabre Ladies:

Dark Carnival

Step right up, folks, to a show, unlike anything you've ever seen before. Circus terrors and frights, sure to delight. Here at Dark Carnival, we've got it all.

Freaks and clowns, screams and laughter and always, a healthy side of the macabre.

So, come one, come all and join us, if you dare

Welcome to the Show.

For upcoming releases, you can follow us on Facebook or our website.

As always, thanks for reading. Until next time!

xxx

Eleanor Merry and Cassandra Angler

The Macabre Ladies

https://macabreladies.wixsite.com/website

https://www.facebook.com/groups/macabreladies